THE MAID

ROBERT LEWIS BARROS, M.D.

THE MAID

ROBERT LEWIS BARROS, M.D.

CITIOFBOOKS, INC.
3736 Eubank NE Suite A1
Albuquerque, NM 87111-3579
www.citiofbooks.com
Hotline: 1 (877) 389-2759
Fax: 1 (505) 930-7244

Ordering Information:
Quantity sales. Special discounts are available on quantity purchases by corporations, associations, and others. For details, contact the publisher at the address above.

Printed in the United States of America.

ISBN-13:	Softcover	979-8-89391-247-0
	Hardcover	979-8-89391-248-7
	eBook	979-8-89391-249-4

Library of Congress Control Number: 2024916641

*DEDICATED TO MY DEAR
MOM ORFI*

Contents

1. Title
2. Copyright
3. Dedication
4. The Maid

How the years go by so fast. I remember when Mr. Julio Del Rey Baron and Mrs. Andrea Castillo Del Rey were still alive. What a beautiful place to grow up it was. I was one of the servants that grew up in this palace. The houses are still in back where all the different families lived that made the castle function so many years ago. It was like a small village; many families are still there. Mrs. Del Rey was the daughter of the King of Spain; Mr. Del Rey, her husband, was her cousin.

My name is Margarita. This is our story. I grew up in this incredible, beautiful, romantic, mysterious, huge Spanish castle. Well, not exactly in it, my Mom worked for the Del Rey family. She cleaned the bedrooms and the bathroom in the castle; there were many of them.

We were some of the servants that kept this gigantic castle functioning. There were fifty-two of us, not counting the house servants, or the children. We lived in back and did all the manual labor. We did the cleaning and the cooking. We took care of the farm and planted the vegetables and the fruit and took care of the animals. We cleaned the pools and the fountains and made the flowers bloom in the numerous gardens. We looked after the grape vines and made the wine. We did all the work that was needed. It was truly like a small village.

There were also the house servants. They were the privileged ones. Their job was to serve and give the royal family and friends everything they needed and wanted to enjoy. Even though the servants made all the food in the kitchen, set up for the parties, and did all the work, it was the house servants who opened the door in the castle for the guests and family. The house servants served the food for the guests and friends and family at the table, by the pool, in the garden, or wherever they were needed or were entertaining. They never got their hands dirty. They felt above us, the servants.

We were happy; we needed nothing. Though we were servants, we had our houses. We had our family life. We baked bread for our family. We had holidays together, unless we were needed at the castle on that day. Usually that only involved the servants that had to do with the food and, of course, the house servants. The rest of us were rarely needed during the holidays.

All the house servants wore white gloves. The gloves had to be perfectly white. They had dozens of them in the kitchen. The house servers would frequently change gloves to make sure the gloves were always perfectly white when they served the food. The formal attire had to be outstanding for the house servants.

There were also some women house servants. They were the ones that helped Mrs. Del Rey get dressed, put on her wig, and get her make up on. They helped her with her bath, her perfumes, and to put on her night clothing. Mrs. Del Rey would ring a bell whenever she needed something or someone.

Sometimes when Mrs. Del Rey needed company, she would ring her bell; the house servants would come running. She would dismiss the men, and the women sat around listening to her talk. She loved to talk and have the women house servants listen. She knew no one else in the family would worry about her or come to listen. Her family never wanted to be around her. They did not like her company. All her relatives and friends disliked her. When there was a party and they had to be around her, they were all a bunch of hypocrites and acted like they liked her company; otherwise, they would be out of her social circle. Everybody wanted to be on her guest list, so they always put up with her often unkind behavior.

When she was lonely, she called the house servants. Sometimes she wanted to be kind with them, and she would ask about their children and family and how they were getting along, but then she would start to tell her tales, mostly about her family and her royal friends and relatives. Mrs. Del Rey would talk, and the women house servants would listen as Mrs. Del Rey talked for hours. Sometimes the women would do some embroidering or netting while they listened and occasionally participated in the conversation. Frequently, Mrs. Del Rey would send a house servant to tell the kitchen crew to make tea and some cakes and to ring when they had it ready so that the house servants could come to pick it up.

She told them one day: "Remember Mr. Gerostoni? He was a handsome man, but he was a little devil. He tried to catch my eye a time or two, but I never showed him any interest. Gossip is he died last year. Apparently, his wife found him with his lover in their bed. She shot him through the head, and as his lover was getting up, she shot her through the center of her buttocks." They would all laugh, then she would start another story. It was obvious that she was a very lonely woman that wanted to appear strong and in command always; after all, she was royal. She had no family that wanted to spend the afternoons with. Her royal family and friends mostly disliked her, but she always felt her title was the most important thing.

Meanwhile, in the castle, the attire for men house servants was formal black tuxedos, perhaps with a red or white carnation in the lapel. They had to be very friendly but formal and never lose sight of their place amongst all these aristocrats. They had to remember the names and titles of all family members and guests. Most of the guests called the house servants by their first names. The initial greeting of the guests at the door was often done by the butler. He had to be formal and address the guest by their title or last name. He helped the guest get situated.

The butler had a formal education in accounting and was the one that managed the castle and the finances for the family. He paid all the servants and other providers of goods not made in the property.

The house servants, when they were hired, had to have a certificate that showed they were properly trained by a special institute to be a house servant. It was a profession, and most were house servants for life and were very proud of it. Some were often looked at as if they were part of the family. They were the pride of the house. This was where the family showed off to other family members and friends, the luxury and friendliness they wanted their friends and family to enjoy.

No one in the royal family appeared to have a job. They spent all their time and energy trying to impress and entertain their family and friends. Money never seemed to be a problem. They were always trying to find ways to spend it. They wanted to show that they had the newest and latest and most expensive vacation mansions, toys, horses' food, wine, and entertainment to impress all of the guests and family members that came to visit.

The house servants were very well paid. Not any commoner could be a house servant. They were trained in having proper speech and proper ways to treat and approach the guests. It was a privilege to see how the wealthiest and most sophisticated and influential people lived. Their alternative was to live in poverty with limited food, housing, and clothing for their families.

As a house servant, they were permitted to eat the royal family's food and wine, after all the guests had gone home. They had a lot of time off, because they were not entertaining every day, but almost every day they were entertaining some guests. They did not have to worry about cleaning or making the food or making the beds, and they took turns helping with the daily routine of serving the family and occasional guests, but on the days they had several guests or a party, they all had to be there with their best.

I remember those unforgettable years, remembered Margarita. We were just kids. The royal family Del Rey had two children, Eduardo and Antonio. Eduardo was the oldest. He was very serious and not very social and did not like the neighborhood kids. He liked to play with his cousins and other royal friends. His brother, Antonio, was different. He loved to play with the servants' kids. He was easygoing, playful, and full of life and fun.

The royal parents don't get involved very much with raising their kids. They have house servants do it all. They involved different house servants in the duties of raising their children. These were protocols that were developed generations before by the royal families on how to raise the children. The parents are rarely involved, but the children are very well taken care of, and of course, their every need is looked after. When the children become three years old and begin to walk about, they are assigned a house servant that will always be around them to make sure they are not involved in any activity that might hurt them. This house servant is also responsible for the proper clothing they need to wear. They help with toilet issues. Also, as a member of the royal family, there are always protocols about what they should wear to family and official events. This caretaker will take them to the tailor to have the proper clothing and uniforms made that, as a member of the royal family, they are required to wear. He knows what clothing they are permitted to wear. He has to make sure their clothing is always perfectly clean before they sit at the dinner table. After all, they are royal, and they have to learn how to dress and act and speak and how to deal with the older generation of royal members of the family. They have to learn what their place is in the family as they grow up and integrate into the family. It is a whole process of learning your place and the proper behavior as a part of the royal family. As they get older, these individuals become your lifelong friends. When Antonio was three years old, Pablo was assigned to look after Antonio, and Guillermo was assigned to look after Eduardo. Pablo and Guillermo had to go through six months of training in a special institute to learn their job. It was usually a lifelong commitment, and as Antonio and Eduardo got older, they became lifelong friends.

The Del Rey family had a history that went back several generations.

Back in those years, when two countries formalized an alliance, it was very common to seal the deal with family ties. Often not only having a political alliance but also having a family seal. This made for a stronger union between the two countries. In this case, the alliance was between Spain and Portugal. The king of Portugal's son, Carlos Del Rey the Fourth, had married Christina Natalia Castillo. The arrangement was that the married couple would come to live in Spain. Several generations later, Mr. Del Rey's family, as luck would have it, had not kept a close family parentage to the royal families in Spain. Andrea, Mrs. Del Rey, was the daughter of the king of Spain, but Julio, Mr. Del Rey, was a distant cousin to Andrea and the Spanish royal family. His family, however, had maintained close family parentage to the royal family in Portugal. The castle where Julio and Andrea lived belonged to the Del Rey family for generations.

Mrs. Del Rey was very conscious of her social status and did not like her children playing with the servants' kids; however, Mr. Del Rey would always say, "Oh Andrea, they are just kids; let them play together."

Mr. Del Rey was easygoing, kind, and loved to laugh and dance. He enjoyed life to the fullest. Mr. Del Rey treated people well and respected their dignity. He never made them feel like he was above them. Mrs. Del Rey, on the other hand, complained about everything. She was unkind to us, "the servants," and all of us were afraid of her. She often humiliated us. Mr. Del Rey just ignored her. She was grouchy and unhappy all the time. Nothing seemed to please her. She was very conscious of her social status, and she wanted everyone to know it, especially her friends and family. They all went along with her because they knew well that she was the one that had the money, the power, and the social status. If you wanted to be in her social circle, you had to kiss her ass and put up with her crap, and she let you know it.

We were just children as we observed from a distance the behavior of this somewhat dysfunctional family, remembered Margarita.

We never played with Eduardo. He felt he was above us. He seemed unhappy all the time. We loved to play with Antonio. He was one of us. We would run around in the gardens and in the fields with him, playing like children often do, but Margarita was his favorite. Frequently we would have neighborhood races and other contests and competitions, and Antonio and Margarita always won. Antonio, who was muscular and tall and very strong, would always let Margarita win. Margarita would challenge him in so many physical events, climbing trees, jumping off the rope into the river, swimming across the river, and, of course, Antonio would always let Margarita win. Antonio, however, was aware of just how talented physically Margarita was, and of course, this made for a better friendship. Though she was a strong swimmer, she knew that Antonio would always let her win. They played in the water, they ran in the mud, and they loved being together. They admired each other so much. Sometimes, Antonio would climb to a branch of the tree that was overlooking the river and would jump and do a flip before landing on the deep river. When she complained that he might get hurt, he would say: "I am not doing this to show off; I am really doing it because I want to share my most intimate secrets with you." They loved each other's company. They saw each other every day, and when they couldn't see each other, they missed each other terribly. It was part of their daily routine. Of course, it was common that as soon as Antonio would come to play with us, he would yell out "Margarita," and Margarita would run out of the house to play with him.

Margarita was a very happy, energetic, and expressive child. She exploded with enthusiasm. She ran dawn the garden corridors with her arms open, singing some happy tune. She looked like a bird that was about to take off in flight at any moment. She was always dancing, singing, and jumping around. All the kids admired her; she was so beautiful and had very good self-esteem, and though she was Antonio's favorite, she always treated the rest of us with kindness and respect. She was truly beautiful inside and out. Dancing seemed to be her passion. Though there was no music, she would sing and dance her own happy tunes. She often seemed to be in charge of the group and appeared smarter than all of us. Sometimes, she was in her own little world, but when Antonio would show up, the two of them would often take off and play together.

Margarita was one year younger than Antonio; she was definitely his favorite. He always told Margarita that she was beautiful and that someday he was going to marry her. Every time he came out to play, he would pick a flower from the garden, and he would bring it to her.

As the years passed, Antonio and Margarita's friendship improved. Antonio never made Margarita feel like he was above her or above any of us, the servants. His mother would get angry every time she would see us playing with Antonio. She would get angry with Pablo and threatened to dismiss him. She would tell Antonio to go in the house and that she never wanted to see him playing with the servants' kids again. Mrs. Del Rey would often come to Margarita's house and yell at her parents and would say that she was going to fire them if she ever found out that Margarita was playing with Antonio again. Margarita's mother would punish Margarita, but that never affected Antonio or Margarita from playing together. When Antonio went out to play, Pablo would look out to make sure Mrs. Del Rey would not find them. Antonio would sneak by Margarita's house, and Margarita would run out, and they would go to their hiding place to play. They talked about being together always.

Antonio spent every morning with his tutors. There were two of them that taught them from eight in the morning until noon. They taught them to read and write Spanish and English. They taught them math and science, music, art, history. They also taught them the proper behavior and the titles and the parentage of the members of the royal family.

Margarita also went to a nearby public school every morning. It was a public school for the less fortunate at the nearby village. It was in the afternoon that Margarita and Antonio spent much of their time together. By now, they were just nine and ten years old, but they really loved spending time together. They would climb trees, go to the stables, and the two of them would secretly jump on a horse bareback. They played hide and seek. When Margarita's birthday would come, Antonio would secretly ask the cook to make Margarita a cake. Antonio would place flowers around the cake and bring it to her. They would take it to their hiding place to eat it together. The two of them would feed the pigeons and the birds. Pablo was always looking out for them, making sure his mother did not find them. Antonio was a loving and kind person. As they got older, Antonio would hold Margarita's hand and tell her that he was going to marry her when they were older.

When Antonio was a child, he did not know that his marriage had already been arranged. This was a normal procedure for the royal families.

The years passed, and when Antonio was fourteen years old, his parents sent Antonio and his brother to a boarding school for the royals and the rich and famous. Margarita was very sad when she heard Antonio was going away.

Some years before, she had found a small rock in the nearby river. It was a crystalline, beautiful, shining rock. She always thought it was a precious stone. She had never seen anything like it, and it was something very dear and precious to her. It was really her treasure. When Antonio was going away to boarding school, he came to say goodbye. Margarita took her precious stone and gave it to Antonio. She said: "This is my most precious treasure. I want you to have it so you will remember me. I know I will think about you every day," she said.

Antonio said: "I wish I didn't have to go. It's going to be hard for me not seeing you. You are my best and dearest friend." He took the stone and looked at it and said: "This is really beautiful. I have never seen anything so beautiful.

She said: "I found it in the river years ago, and now I want you to have it." He took her hand and kissed the back of it. Margarita let a tear sneak out.

Antonio turned his head and said: "I have to go."

Margarita started helping her mother more with the cleaning of the mansion's bedrooms and bathrooms. Vacations would come along, and Antonio would come by, and he would love to call out "Margarita." Suddenly her heart would jump with joy, and she would come running out to see her loving friend. Every time Margarita would see Antonio, he looked taller and more handsome. Every time Antonio saw Margarita, she seemed more beautiful and charming and graceful in her own gentle way. Antonio loved to bring her flowers. Margarita loved the time they were together. Every time he came home, they would spend hours talking, sharing their secrets and stories.

Arranged marriages were always a part of the royal families' culture and way of life. They thought they had to maintain the royal blood pure, and not permit outsiders to contaminate the linage of the royal family's blood. Unfortunately, scientifically speaking, this was a great error on their part.

Being related, especially if you are closely related, means that you probably have a similar gene pool which occasional bring the defective genes together, bringing genetic abnormalities.

It is a little complicated, but when you are of the same family, you tend to have a similar gene pool. Most genetic disorders are caused when defective genes are passed from both sides of the family. That is why it is against the law in most countries to marry someone of your own family. In most countries, you must be at least four generations removed to be able to marry that person. Having a similar gene pool, you have a greater chance of passing similar recessive genes that may cause genetic disorders.

In the Spanish royal families, it was somewhat common to have an "opa" hidden somewhere in the castle. An opa is an individual that has been born with a genetic disorder that makes him undesirable in his appearance or his mental capacity or physical ability or both. Sometimes when one of these opa children were born, they were sacrificed and claimed they died of some accident. When there was this genetic defect, it was fairly common for the mother and the defective child to die during childbirth.

Margarita didn't know that Antonio had an arranged marriage with Antonio's cousin Britana. Now that he was getting older, his mother was pushing Antonio into having a better relationship with his cousin Britana. Antonio's mother would make him call on her at her house so they would get better acquainted.

Antonio hated her with all his heart. He finally told Margarita about his arranged marriage. He would tell Margarita that Britana was ugly and no fun to be with. He told Margarita that there was no way they were going to make him marry Britana.

Frequently, Britana's family would come to spend the afternoon with the Del Rey family, trying to develop a closer family relationship. Poor Margarita would peak through the windows, and she would shed tears as she watched the parents make Antonio sit next to Britana.

When she heard of the arranged marriage, her heart was crushed, but she did not lose hope; in her heart, she believed that Antonio would spend the rest of his life with her. She believed him when he told her that he wanted a family with her, and no one was going to make him marry Britana.

Antonio's mother would get angry with Antonio because she noticed that he did not have any enthusiasm for Britana.

Arranged marriages have always taken place in the Spanish royal families, and it was Antonio's duty to respect this family tradition and the promises made had to be honored. These were commitments that had always existed and never questioned and had to be accepted and respected concerning arranged marriages.

Antonio's father had been an arranged marriage, and Mr. Julio had to live with the consequences. Years before, when Julio was four years old, Julio's parents had accepted the marriage arrangement with Andrea because Andrea was from a higher social status in Spain. Antonio's father, Mr. Julio Del Rey, had been a beautiful, likeable child, always smiling energetic, and happy. Everyone would say, "Look, what a beautiful child." That is why, though he was not as high in the "royal" social scale, Andrea's parents had chosen Julio to marry Andrea, because he was a likeable child. Andrea, on the other hand, had been a grouchy, spoiled, and difficult child. She was two years older than Julio, but she had no takers in the Spanish royal family, so her family accepted the marriage with Julio. Of course, Julio's family was delighted to have their son marry Andrea, the daughter of the king, but Julio had to live with the consequences. Poor Julio had no say in the deal. Andrea's family were in a hurry to find a match for Andrea, and though she was two years older than Julio, they wanted to get Andrea married off.

Back in those days, divorce was not an option for the members of the Spanish royal family. They often had lovers, but a divorce was impossible. Antonio knew how unhappy his father had been with Andrea. He had seen the sad and unkind treatment his mother had towards his father, and as he became older, it became more obvious. If he married Britana, who was the daughter of the kings' son, she would be higher in the royal social scale than Antonio. He would be looking to a possible unhappy marriage like his father. Antonio did not want to admit, however, that unlike his mother, Britana seemed to be a gentle, attractive, happy, likeable, kind, and friendly girl.

Years kept passing, and when Antonio was leaving for the university in Madrid, he kissed Margarita passionately for the first time. They knew they wanted each other. Margarita's heart was sealed, and she would never ever permit anyone to touch her heart again. Antonio gave Margarita a golden pendent. From a golden chain hung a golden heart with a diamond in the center. Antonio said to her: "This is my heart; you have it now. Only you will ever have my heart. Keep it next to your heart and never take it off." They both hugged each other, and with tears, Antonio was off to the university.

Antonio's parents had bought Antonio a brand-new red sports car as a graduation present since he was such good student. They had the car made in England where they were specialists in sports cars for the rich and famous. Sports cars were rare in Spain at that time. The car was made specifically for Antonio and shipped to Spain. It had Antonio's name on it.

Antonio was very good looking, and through his high school years, the girls were always after him. Margarita could see it, because frequently, when the royal family had parties for their son's birthdays and other families' social events in the mansion, Margarita would hide and peak through the windows to see what was going on in these fancy parties, with all these aristocratic friends and royal relatives. She would see how the girls would just go after Antonio, but he always behaved, and of course, Britana would be there to hold his hand and chase the girls away.

As the years passed, Antonio's mother would always ask him to take Britana home after the parties, and Margarita would see them going off in Antonio's new red sports car. Margarita could only hold on to the golden heart pendent that Antonio had given her. Her heart was aching, and all she could do was cry.

When these aristocratic young men went off to college, it was an opportunity for them to have their adventures before they went into marriage and have a family. Most of them were going into arranged marriages as well, and this was their time to sow their wild oats. All these young men were privileged and had new cars, perfect clothing, and of course, many of the girls were taken by them.

Vacations would come, and Antonio would always come by Margarita's house and yell like he did years ago when they were children. "Margarita!" he would yell. She would hold on to her golden heart pendent and would come out running.

Antonio would tell Margarita that he was going to marry Britana, whom he hated. The wedding would take place when he finished college. Margarita couldn't hide her tears.

Margarita and Antonio would go to their hiding place and climb the old maple tree near the barn. They would climb up to their favorite branch, and the two of them would straddle the branch facing each other. They would talk for hours, catching up about their activities, trying to avoid the topic of Britana. Antonio would ask Margarita: "Do you want to go for a ride in my sport car?"

Margarita would say, "What if they see us?"

Antonio would say, "I don't care; you are really my love. You have always been and always will be, since I was six years old, when I saw you dancing in front of your house, and I said to myself: Someday I am going to marry that girl,' and now I am heartbroken because it was just a dream, but I want you to know that no matter what happens, you hold in your hand my heart."

Several years before, Mr. Julio and Eduardo had been visiting the royal family in Portugal. When Eduardo was four years old, he had developed a special friendship with his cousin Elizabeth. She was the daughter of Julio's sister. Mr. Julio had formalized a marriage arrangement between Eduardo and Elizabeth. When Eduardo, who was older than Antonio, had turned twenty-two, he married his cousin Elizabeth.

One year later, Eduardo and Elizabeth had a beautiful baby girl, Marina.

When Antonio turned twenty-two years old, he finished college, and the family prepared for the upcoming wedding. All the royal families attended. His brother and his family and other cousins from Portugal had come for the royal wedding. Though Britana was delighted with the marriage, it was obvious that Antonio was not so happy.

It was the custom amongst the royal families in Spain that, on the night of the wedding, the couple used a special sheet when they make love so that when the women's hymen was broken and the bride bleeds, the blood went into the sheet, and the next morning, the sheet was placed in a special place outside their honeymoon suite for all to see that the bride was a virgin and intercourse had taken place. Of course, Margarita was heartbroken when she saw the bloody sheet, but Antonio did what he had to do.

Britana moved into the palace where they had prepared a special place for them.

Margarita, who had graduated from high school some years back, continued to help her aging mother change the sheets on the beds and wash the sheets and towels. As time passed, she could not help but to see Britana occasionally in the halls of the palace. Margarita would notice that Britana was pregnant.

Antonio and Margarita had very little contact during this time. Antonio was afraid that if his mother became aware of the great love and admiration he had for Margarita, his mother would fire Margarita, and he would not be able to see her anymore. Antonio was in a difficult spot. He was married to Britana, but his heart was with Margarita. He could not figure out how to resolve this difficult problem that made his heart ache every day. When he made love to Britana, he would dream of being with Margarita. He often went for long walks wondering what it would be like to live with his love, Margarita. He felt like he was in prison, unable to live the life he had dreamt off since he was a child.

Antonio decided to confide to his father, hoping to find some comfort. His father understood his dilemma. He would tell his father that his problem was more complicated now that Britana was pregnant. He told his father how he had always dreamt of having a family with Margarita. How since childhood they had promised their love. He told him how his soul ached every day. He said that he avoided seeing Margarita because he knew that it would only bring more sadness to both of them. He told his father that sometimes he felt like he has ruined Margarita's life, because she would never be able to have a family. She would never experience what it feels like to be a mother. "I know her well," he said. "She has pledged her love to me, and I know she will never break that pledge. I pledged my love to her, and I broke the pledge, and I know she hurts every day, and I don't know how to fix it."

One day, Antonio had invited his friend Raul to spend the night at the palace. Raul was the son of his mother's friend Victoria. They had known each other since they were four years old. They had gone to college together. They had been on the same soccer team. They had traveled together, and their families knew each other well. Raul, Antonio, and Britana had gone to a formal event together. Antonio had invited Raul to stay in his house for the night, since Raul lived further away.

Margarita was placing the finishing touches in the guest suite. She placed the flowers on top of the dresser; she brought out the fragrance and the clean towels where Raul, Antonio's friend, was going to spend the night.

Normally, the protocol was that the servant that makes the bed and prepares the room had no contact with the guest. The house servants normally carry the bags to the guestroom and show the guest to their room.

Raul looked through the window and saw beautiful Margarita preparing the room. He then, without the proper invitation or protocol, went up to the room and proceeded to rape Margarita. Margarita tried to scream, but he put a towel in her mouth. He then violently raped Margarita. When he was done, he left the room, and Margarita cried out. Mrs. Andrea came running out. Margarita told her what had happen. Mrs. Del Rey fired Margarita on the spot and told Raul not to worry, she was just a maid.

It was common for the royal men to take advantage of the servants in that way. They always thought they could do whatever they wanted, whenever they wanted, with the servants without consequences. However, the honorable gentlemen would never have this kind of behavior, and it was rare for this to happen inside the house. They usually would take them somewhere else, often offer them money, and rarely end up with a rape, and if it happened that they raped them, it was better for the servant that was raped to keep quiet about it, because it would almost always would result in their dismissal. It was common for these royal men to have children with these young girls; sometimes the girls were only thirteen or fourteen years old. At times, these royal men would raise these children in their own homes or sometimes would be raised by grandparents or other relatives. These children grew up in a sad environment in which they were hated by the woman of the house, the wife. They were often treated as a cross between a servant and an undesirable family member.

The rapist may have some pity for the family and the fourteen-year-old child he raped and occasionally would help out with some of the newborn child's expenses. Often, however, they would act like nothing happen and would negate the whole thing. Occasionally, some of them would take full responsibility and pay the family all the expenses so that their son or daughter could have a good life.

During that time in Spain, the women who had a child without a marriage were seen as a promiscuous woman, and no one wanted anything to do with this dishonorable person. They were looked down by their family and friends, and it was difficult for them to survive.

Margarita was devastated and crying, sitting on the floor against the wall, when Antonio entered the room. Antonio noticed the blood on the bed, and on Margarita's torn gown. There was blood running down Margarita's leg. He could see the bruising of the violent rape that had taken place. He found the heart pendent he had given Margarita torn on top of the bed. He picked up the bloody pendent, and he said to Margarita, "I am going to do something about this." Antonio's heart was crushed beyond repair. He could hardly hide the tears.

Mrs. Del Rey said to Antonio: "Nothing happened; Raul was in his room, and Margarita made advances towards him, and Raul had intercourse with her. No big deal, she is just a maid. I have already fired Margarita, and I am going to tell her family to leave also, right away."

Antonio said to his mother: "Mother, have you no decency no morals, no sense of right or wrong, no honor that you can permit this to happen in our house, the temple of honor? I am going to do something about this right now," Antonio said again.

Antonio, Britana, and Raul had just attended a formal event, and they all were wearing formal attire. They had just arrived from a wedding party before all of this happened.

After the rape, Antonio said to Raul: "Come into my office right now; I want to speak with you." Antonio said to Raul: "You don't come to this our house to dishonor and disgrace our home in this way." Antonio took his white gloves and slapped Raul's face. Antonio than told Raul: "Get your things and get out of my house."

The fact that Antonio had slapped Raul's face with his white gloves meant that he was challenging Raul to a duel.

His mother couldn't believe it. Mrs. Del Rey said to Antonio: "Are you going to put your life in danger or kill your childhood friend over a maid, a servant?"

Antonio told his mother that he must bring honor to their home. He said, "Raul has disgraced our house. What Raul has done in this our house is barbaric, indecent, disrespectful, and dishonorable, and there must be honor in this house. Mother, I am really surprised that you approve of such barbaric behavior and act like she was an animal without any rights or respect," said Antonio. "I can't accept this kind of behavior in our house."

Margarita and her family are ushered out of the property. The family was given their severance pay for the years of work and dedication to the Del Rey family.

Margarita and her family took the train to Barcelona to live with some relatives.

Margarita felt bad that her family had to be fired because of her. She felt guilty. Her family let her know that she had brought disgrace upon the family. Margarita's father threw her out of the house. He told her that they never ever want to see her again.

Margarita was twenty-two years old, and she needed a job so she could live away from her family that blamed her for the sadness that had come to her and her family.

Margarita spent days living in the park, eating out of trash cans. She fought off the men who again and again were trying to take advantage of her. She was devastated. She couldn't find a solution. She sat on a bench in the park and started to cry. She was considering suicide; her eyes were swollen from all the crying. She didn't know what to do.

A lady that was passing by noticed the devastation of poor Margarita. She was so gorgeous, though her clothing were dirty; she has not had a bath in a long time, still Margarita was so beautiful, and the lady couldn't understand why she cried and looked so sad. The lady asked Margarita why she was so sad and destroyed. Margarita was embarrassed to tell her what was going on in her life. The lady told Margarita, "My name is Ana, and I just got off work. I live around the corner; why don't you come with me to my house? We'll have some coffee, and you can tell me all about your problem."

Margarita told her: "No, I don't want to bother you. I'll be okay."

Ana said, "It's no bother, and you look like you could use a friend." Margarita and Ana went to Ana's house. Ana made some coffee and said to Margarita: "Come, sit, tell me what makes you so sad."

Margarita said, "I am too embarrassed to tell you."

"Ana asked, "Tell me, what your name is?" She said, "Margarita."

"We all have problems, and I want to help you," said Ana. "I don't think you can help me," responded Margarita.

Ana said, "It will do you good to talk about it." Margarita began to tell Ana her sad story of the rape and how her family had been dismissed from their job that they had for so many years, and now they had to find a way to survive. She also told her how she needed to find a job desperately. Her family had blamed her for this disgrace and had thrown her out of the house.

Ana said to Margarita, "You see, it is a good thing you told me about your problem. There is always a solution. I work for Mr. Gray's family. I am the cook. Mr. Gray and his wife are looking for a nanny for their three children. They are very nice people, and tomorrow we can talk to them to see if they will give you the job. You can stay with me until you get a job. Tonight, you take a long bath, and let's see if we can find you some clothing that will fit you."

Margarita got out of the bath; her long hair was wrapped up in a towel. Ana brought several dresses that used to fit her when she was younger and slimmer. "You can have them all," she said. "Here," said Ana, "try them on."

"Are you sure you want me to have them? They are very beautiful," said Margarita.

"I bought them when my husband was alive, and I was young and slim. He used to buy me everything. He died of lung cancer; he was a chain smoker. Now I must work to support myself. I can't wear them anymore; I am too fat. I had been thinking of giving them to the abused woman's foundation, but I prefer you have them; I think they will fit you. I once was thin and beautiful like you."

"You are still beautiful, inside and out," said Margarita. Margarita tried on the dresses, and they all looked gorgeous on her. They were red and blue and white and beige and pink and baby blue and purple. Margarita had not seen such beautiful dresses in her entire life, except for the ones they wore at the castle, and they still were not as beautiful, Margarita thought.

Ana told Margarita to wear the white one tomorrow. "It is more conservative, and you will look more professional. They don't speak Spanish, but we understand each other. After being with them for four years, I have learned a lot of English, and here is my book that I look at every night. The Easy Way to Speak English. It has helped me a lot. By the way, they are looking for a live-in nanny, so they can go out for their many social events; that way, you won't have to look for a place to live. He is the American consulate to Barcelona."

Fortunately, Margarita got the job working for the American family as a nanny taking care of their three children. Mr. Gray, the house owner, was very pleased with Margarita. She seemed like an honorable person, and the kids took to her right away.

Margarita took good care of the children, taught them games, songs, and how to dance. She was always playing with them. The Gray family was delighted with Margarita.

⊷⊷⊷≫≫❦≪≪⊶⊶⊶

Mr. Julio had married Mrs. Andrea when he was only eighteen years old. Andrea's family was concerned to wait much longer because they felt that Andrea, who was two years older than Julio, may be passing her most fertile years if she waited much longer to marry Julio.

At the age of twenty, two years after he married Andrea, Mr. Julio had a problem with a thirty-five-year-old cousin of Andrea; his name was Felipe. Felipe was a grotesque, aggressive, boisterous, self-centered, obese person. He thought he was God's gift to the world. He was always making fun of the people around him and criticizing everyone. They all were very afraid of him. Felipe had killed two previous individuals in duels, and now, no one opposed him in anyway, and they had to put up with his unkind abuses.

One day, Felipe was criticizing Julio's mother and was laughing in front of the family and friends about how Julio's mother dressed and acted. Julio's mother was quiet and shy and very beautiful. The truth was, Felipe had made advances towards her, but she did not accept them, so Felipe started to try and humiliate her. Julio was furious about this and told Felipe that he should not criticize anyone since he was an ugly fat and abusive pig. Felipe challenged twenty-year-old Julio to a duel.

In those days, when you were challenged to a duel and you did not accept, you were branded a coward, and people did not have any respect for you. The royal families and aristocrats always resolved their problems with a duel. Only the commoners went outside to fight with their fists.

Felipe was married to a fifteen-year-old girl, Regina. Regina's father, Edward, had died two years before of cancer of the prostate, and his family had taken all of the family's fortune. This left Regina's mother and Regina with little money to survive.

Regina's mother, Bruselda, had married an English duke, Edward, the Duke of Comonwell. Edward had visited the royal family in Spain and had fallen in love with Bruselda. They were married a year later. After living five years in Spain, the couple moved back to London where they lived until Edward died. Bruselda and Edward had been unable to have a child; however, at the age of thirty-eight, Bruselda was finally able to have a baby girl they named Regina.

The duke had a previous family and had four children, Charles and Peter and Nicole and Francesca. His previous wife died of pneumonia. Edward was twenty years older than Bruselda. The duke's family had opposed the marriage with Bruselda from the start, and from the beginning, they showed their discontent. The duke had been forced by his family to ask Bruselda to sign a prenuptial agreement, excluding her from any of the duke's fortune. Edward's family, who opposed the marriage, had obligated Edward as a condition of marriage to Bruselda that he ask for this agreement.

Bruselda's family were very wealthy, and she had been brought up with all the privileges of money and power. Money was never an issue. She was twenty-eight years old, and she had been unable to find a husband. She had been promised to marry her young uncle Romulo. He was only five years older than her. He had gone to Africa in a safari and never came back. The years had passed, and this beautiful twenty-eight-year-old woman remained single.

The duke explained to Bruselda the difficulty he was having with his family about his estate. She told him not to worry; money was not an issue. She just asked that this be kept secret and that her family not be informed of this agreement, which she signed. The duke's family looked down on Bruselda because she was a Spaniard. During the time her husband was alive, he always treated her with love and respect and gave her everything. He loved her with all his heart. She was finally able to have a baby girl that they both adored, Regina. During the time they lived in Spain, Bruselda's father, heard the gossip that had been started by Edward's family. He found out about the agreement she had signed with the duke prior to her marriage. Her father was furious and humiliated and insulted. He disinherited Bruselda. This caused a lot of friction in the family, and this was the reason that they had to move to London, after five years of living in Spain.

In London, things were not any better. They excluded Regina and her mother from any birthday parties and family events. Edward was always fighting with his children of his first marriage. Bruselda and the duke were isolated from both sides of the family. Poor Regina grew up without any family contact. They, however, were able to live a life of wealth and privilege.

One day, the duke noticed he was having some problems urinating, and he went to see his physician. Upon examination, the doctor had found a hard mass during a rectal exam. He told Edward that he had prostate cancer. The doctor told him that he didn't know how long he would live, but he said there was no cure, and it was a good idea to put his life in order.

Edward went home to Bruselda, and they both cried together. The duke started to slowly move money into an account in a Geneva bank in Bruselda's name; however, when the family found out that the duke had cancer, they began to control the money, as his health started to deteriorate rapidly. He started losing weight. The cancer began to spread into other organs. He became short of breath and was having some confusion before he finally died.

It didn't take long before the duke's family intimidated and humiliated Bruselda, and before she permitted that, she decided to move back to Spain. In Spain, things were worse. Family members would say, "That's what happens to you when you humiliate our family." She was isolated and didn't know where to turn. She became worried and unhappy. She worried for poor Regina who was being snubbed by her family.

Her husband had left her some money in the Geneva banks, but it was not enough for Regina and her mother to continue living in the style of life they had been used to. Bruselda worried that the money would not be enough to see her through the years she had left.

That is when Felipe came into the picture. He had just lost his wife. He, too, had children from a previous marriage. Regina was only fourteen years old when Felipe discovered the situation they were in. He saw beautiful Regina and a perfect opportunity.

Felipe offered them a life of wealth. He would repair their reputation, and they would once again be accepted into royalty.

When Regina saw Felipe, she begged her mother not to accept the offer. She cried all the time. She told her mother that she deserved to marry a man she would fall in love with, as she had always dreamt. Her mother told her that she had to make a sacrifice; it was the only way they were going to survive.

So, to resolve the money problems that they were going through, Regina's mother forced her fourteen-year-old daughter to marry Felipe, so they could have a better life. He married her six months after his first wife had died. Poor Regina was only fourteen years old when she had to live with this grotesque, complicated, egotist, obese man; he soon began to be her nightmare.

Regina, now fifteen years old, hated Felipe with all her heart. He was so abusive to her and often humiliated her. Felipe liked to go to the whorehouse where he got involved with prostitutes, often coming home late at night, drunk and abusive and belligerent. Bringing venereal diseases home. Regina hated having sex with him because he was so ruff and unkind and brutal and fat. Regina knew nothing about sex; she was just a girl, and she needed someone who was gentle, loving, and a kind lover to teach her how to make love. She hated the painful experience and hated sex, often having to put up with Felipe's alcoholic breath. Felipe had brought home to Regina gonorrhea; this had caused her to have pelvic inflammatory decease, or PID. Because she had no treatment, her fallopian tubes scared down, making her infertile. Felipe was always angry with her because she could not get pregnant, but it was his fault that poor Regina could not get pregnant.

In fact, most of the people in his family and friends hated Felipe, except maybe his two sons he had during his first marriage. The third son died with his mother during childbirth.

They were all in the anticipation to see what was going to happen in this duel between this thirty-five-year-old man very experienced with dueling, and this twenty-year-old boy.

Dueling always had a very specific protocol that had to be followed between the representatives of both parties. They went through all the rules that included the place, the date, the time, and the weapons.

Fortunately, though Julio was inexperienced and so young, Julio believed in himself and was confident that he would prevail. When the time came, though Julio was injured in his upper right arm, he was able to put a bullet right through Felipe's heart. Even though this was accepted and admired by most, some felt that there would be revenge towards him as Felipe's sons got older. Both of his sons seem to have their father's temperament and hated Julio for what he had done to their father. Of course, Julio did what he had to do. He had no choice.

⚜

Antonio began to prepare for his upcoming duel with Raul. Dueling was illegal in Spain, but the royal and aristocratic families did what they wanted. The laws did not seem to apply to them, and dueling had always been a part of their culture to resolve problems whenever their honor or the honor of their family was in question.

Antonio's father had always prepared Eduardo and Antonio to use the dueling pistols in case they would be obligated to bring respect to their families or their personal honor. Mr. Julio was 100 percent in agreement with the decision his son Antonio had made. Antonio did not know until his father showed him the scar and told him the story of how Julio, when he was just twenty years old, and he had to defend his mother's honor when a first cousin of his wife, Felipe, was spreading gossip about his mother.

Mr. Del Rey had an area behind the mansion where they would frequently practice with the dueling pistols. He thought Antonio how to stand for the duel, standing sideways to expose as little as possible of his body to his enemy. He told him that he had to show much confidence, especially in front of Raul. "Let him know that you are ready, and you know you will prevail."

Mr. Del Rey acted as Antonio's representative. The date and the time and place were agreed by both parties. Antonio had placed the golden heart pendent that he had found on the bed the day Margarita had been raped, inside his left shirt pocket. He wanted her to be close to his heart. He knew he was doing this because Raul had hurt him to the core and had hurt and humiliated his only love. When the moment came, Antonio was able to put a bullet through Raul's forehead. This brought great sadness for Antonio, but he knew he did the right thing.

After the dueling episode, Antonio tried to find Margarita. He asked all the servants if they knew where she had gone. No one seemed to know, until one of the servants remembered that the Gonzales family had some relatives in Barcelona. Antonio tried to find her and, finally, was able to find her relatives and her family. Antonio asked about Margarita, and Margarita's father told Antonio that she had left, and they did not know where she had gone. He said that she had disgraced their family and they never wanted to see her again. Antonio tried to explain that what had happened was not Margarita's fault, but they were not able to accept Antonio's story.

⫷⫸

Margarita, unfortunately, had gotten pregnant during this rape episode. Soon, she began to show and had to explain to the Gray family what had happened. Fortunately, Ana talked to Mr. Gray and told him the sad story, and the Gray family reacted positively. They told Margarita that they would see her trough the pregnancy and would help her with everything she needed. The Gray family were very kind and understanding. When the baby girl was born, Margarita called her Estrellita Gonzales.

Everybody called her Este. Margarita did not want to give her daughter the last name of Raul's family; she just gave her own last name.

All the Gray family were very excited with little Este. They took turns holding her; they bought diapers and milk for her and whatever the baby needed.

Mr. Gray had finished his five-year term as a consulate in Barcelona and was going back to his hometown, New York City. He and his wife asked Margarita if she wanted to come to the US with them. Margarita thought this would be a great opportunity for her to leave all her sad past behind and start a new life. She accepted the invitation, and they brought her and the baby to New York with them.

⚜

Some years had passed, and Antonio felt very bad that he killed Raul. He wondered if he made the right decision when he made the decision to have a duel with Raul. Raul's mother, Mrs. Victoria Medina, had just lost her husband to cancer of the colon, and Raul was her only son. Antonio decided to visit Mrs. Victoria to give her his condolences. He wanted to explain why he had made such a drastic decision with his old friend. Antonio drove to Granada in his red sports car where Mrs. Victoria lived.

It was a beautiful spring morning; the flowers were enjoying the morning sun. Antonio put the top down in his sports car, but the only thing that was on his mind was what he was going to say to Mrs. Victoria. He arrived at the plaza in Granada and parked under the shade of a big, old tree in the corner of the plaza; he was trying to collect his thoughts.

Suddenly, he heard someone say: "Master Antonio, what are you doing in Granada?" said Nelly.

"Hi, Nelly," said Antonio, "I haven't seen you around the house in years."

"I had to leave," said Nelly. "I got pregnant, and my parents kicked me out. See that boy shining shoes?" she asked. "That is my son, David." Antonio got out of the car and stepped into the plaza to have a better look. "I got pregnant when your friend Raul raped me. Every time he came to visit your family, we all had to hide. He would even come inside the house and force himself on us. My parents blamed me and kicked me out. I came to live with my cousin Marcela. She is very poor, and I have no way to work or make any money. I have no skills, so I ended up working as a prostitute in the whorehouse over in the red district, I am ashamed to tell you. I have no other way to survive. The men who come to this place, sometimes they pay us, sometimes they don't. They always mistreat us, hurt us, and force themselves upon us, and they end up doing what they want with us. They are often drunk and belligerent, but it is the only way I can survive. It is a terrible life. I only tell you because you were always kind to us, and we felt you were our true friend. I have no one else I can talk to about this. I remember when we were growing up how much we all admired you. We always felt you were one of us. We had so much fun back in those days. I never thought I would end up this way," said Nelly. "I thought I would always live in the castle and marry Castro. He loved me, and I loved him. We were waiting to finish high school, and this disaster happened. Poor Castro, he wanted to marry me anyway, but his family would not permit it."

"You know, your mother knew about Raul," said Nelly. "She always covered up for him. His mother, Mrs. Victoria, also knew. He has ruined many girls' lives. He never took responsibility for what he did. There are some kids that are his children here in Granada. He would not only rape us, but he also enjoyed being violent with us. That gave him great pleasure. I heard what happened to Margarita, and I heard about the duel. Most everybody knows. You did us a great favor. We all think he got what he deserved. It is sad that so many people knew, like Mrs. Del Rey, and did nothing to protect us. They all thought he was so good looking and a real playboy, and many of these older women admired that in him, but he ruined so many of our lives. We were only thirteen or fourteen years old. I think that was his favored age."

"That is so sad," said Antonio. I never knew anything about this. How old is your son?"

"He is twelve years old. This happened to me before it happened to Margarita."

Antonio said, "I am going to take David home to live with Britana and me. We will try to give him a good home and a good education."

"That is so kind of you, Master Antonio. I am so happy I met with you. I never in my dreams thought I would find you here, and I am so happy you will take David. He has practically lived on the streets for some time now. He has been independent for a while. He makes his own money to survive, and he makes his own decisions. He does not listen to me anymore. Everybody thinks that I am a bad mother, but when the word got out that I was pregnant without a husband or a father for my son, they looked down on me, and I couldn't even get a job as a servant. Even my cousin's family looks down on me. They think I did something to provoke the rape. It is such a disgrace.

"Master Antonio, you never told me, what are you doing in Granada?" "Oh, it's a personal matter," said Antonio. "I want to meet David and see

if I can take him home with me."

"I want to be honest with you," said Nelly. "David has been doing drugs. And as I told you, he lives on the street and has some bad friends. They all live under the bridge. I think two of them are his brothers. They are Raul's sons."

"I'll take him home with me. We will give him a good home and see if we can turn his life around."

"David," she called out.

"What do you want? Money?" said David.

"Come here for a minute," said Nelly. "Come here, I want to talk to you." He put his shoe shining box strap over his shoulder and walked towards his mother.

"What do you want?" he asked.

"This is Master Antonio; he wants to take you home with him and give you a good home and an opportunity to have better life."

"I don't want to go," said David. "I like my life just fine. I like my independence. I do what I want, and I don't want anyone telling me what to do."

"I know you have had a sad life," said Nelly, "but this is your opportunity to turn things around. Don't you want a family? People who care about you and give you love, food, education, nice clothing, and place to live?"

"You never cared about me before, and now you want to turn me over to this stranger so he can take advantage of me? No thanks," said

David. "I have all the friends and family I need and want. I am not going with this stranger. No thanks," said David again, then he walked away.

"This is so sad," said Antonio. "I wish I could help." He reached in his pocket and gave Nelly all the money he had with him. Antonio said, "Come by the house; I will talk to my mother and see if we can give you a job."

"No," said Nelly, "my family don't want me anywhere near. Thank you so much, it has been a real pleasure talking to you. Give Princess Britana my love." Nelly walked on.

Antonio did not know what to do. He decided he was going to talk with Mrs. Victoria. He knocked on her door, and the butler opened the door. He recognized Antonio right away. Antonio had visited the house several times. "I want to talk to Mrs. Victoria," said Antonio.

The butler let him in the house and said, "I will be back in a minute." Shortly after, he came back and said, "Mrs. Victoria does not want to see you. She asked me to tell you to please leave." The butler opened the door, and Antonio went out. He got into his car, and he could not hold back the tears. He thought about what Raul had done to his childhood love, the one he had given his heart to. Still, he wondered if he had made the right decision. He thought about Nelly, his old friend, and the sad life she lives. He wondered about Margarita. His heart ached thinking that she might have ended up in a similar sad situation. He remembered her father's anger and how he blamed her for what had happened to her and had thrown her out of the house. He wondered how she was surviving. His tears were flowing out. He couldn't stop crying. Where is my Margarita? he wondered.

⟶⟩⟩⟩❁⟨⟨⟨⟵

Margarita had lost her childhood love. She never thought she could live without him. She decided that it was best for her to leave and let Antonio go on with his family without her interference. In her heart, though she loved him dearly and thought she would never love any one ever again, she thought it was best to let him go on with his family life.

During the time she was in Barcelona with the Gray family, Margarita had made a great effort to learn to speak English. She had formed a tremendous, loving friendship with Gray family. The Gray children, who loved her but spoke no Spanish, made it important, and easier for Margarita to learn to speak English. When the children went to bed, she would study her English book, English in Twenty Minutes. She communicated with all of them, and somehow, she made herself understood. She really became a part of the family. The family could not function without her. She was indispensable. Of course, she also had a very especial friendship with Ana.

The Gray children had teachers that come to their house every day to teach them in English what they needed to know, so when they returned home, they would be able to enter the private school in their corresponding grade. There were professional tutors that worked for the state department that provided this service to the American diplomats.

The sirens were blasting; the ambulance lights were flashing. Everyone got out of the way as the ambulance arrived in Granada. People were wondering what was going on. They all gathered around as the paramedics pick up someone under the bridge. The paramedics noticed that the patient had a slight pulse and no respirations. They intubated him; they noticed he has lost his pulse. They start cardiopulmonary resuscitation.

The ambulance took the patient to the nearest hospital. The Santo Tomas Hospital emergency room, a Catholic hospital.

In the emergency room, they find a young male that has overdosed on narcotics.

They diagnosed his problem right away because the pupils were pinpoint in size, a clear finding with narcotic overdose. The pupils get so small they can hardly be seen.

Unfortunately, the patient was David, Nelly's son. When she found out, she came running to the hospital to find her son, David, in a coma. She hugged him, but there was no reaction. She called his name and asked him to wake up, but David could not react. After CPR, David had recovered his pulse but depended 100 percent on the respirator for oxygenation.

No signs of trauma were found. He had no response to the NARCAN (it is a powerful narcotic antidote; normally it wakes narcotic overdose patients immediately), so they were not completely sure the exact cause of his coma. They did an electroencephalogram. They thought he would be flat line (brain dead), but he did have some electrical activity.

Later, the laboratory confirmed that David had taken a large dose of narcotics. The doctors did not know whether he would recuperate, either partially or completely. If he recovered, it could take months or even years. It was obvious, the NARCAN had been administered too late. He already had brain damage, so he did not wake up.

David was on the respirator for months. They had to do a tracheostomy to keep him on the respirator. Months later, the doctors decided to wean him off the respirator. David continued breathing, slowly at first, and with time, his respirations began to normalize.

He was placed in a small room. The doctors moved him there, waiting for him to die. Every day, Padre Francisco would come to see David; he would kneel next to his bed and hold David's hand and prayed for him.

One day, Padre Francisco found Nelly, who had knelt next to David's bed, praying. Tears were coming down her face as she held the hand of her son. She felt so bad that things had worked out that way. She felt guilty and thought she had been a bad mother. Padre Francisco was surprised to see her there. All of these months had gone by, and no one had ever come to visit David. He asked Nelly who she was. Nelly put her head down and said to him: "I am a shame to tell you that I am David's mother." Padre Francisco took her by the hand, and they went out into the garden where Padre Francisco and Nelly sat down to have a heart-to-heart talk. Nelly began to tell Padre Francisco all about her life and how she got pregnant with David and how she now works in the whorehouse as a prostitute to survive. Padre Francisco told her he knew God has forgiveness for her, and he thought God was going to spare David because God has better plans for David's life. Padre Francisco got Nelly a job cleaning the church.

Mr. Gray was an attorney and was a partner to the firm Gray, Noble, and White. The Gray family were very wealthy. They belonged to the tennis club where they taught the Gray children to play tennis. They were also members of the country club where he played golf every Sunday. Mrs. Gray was very busy; she was running to represent her New York district in the House of Representatives. She wanted to be a congresswoman.

Aside from Margarita, who helped make the sandwiches for the kids and made sure the children were well dressed before they went off to school, the Gray family also had a chuffer and a cook. The children went to private schools and were taken to school by the chuffer. The kids, now in high school, needed very little care from Margarita.

Mr. Gray was a diabetic and had hypertension. The visiting nurse had taught Margarita how to take Mr. Gray's blood pressure. This was done two times daily; Margarita had to record in a special notebook the daily blood pressures taken. That way, when Mr. Gray went to see his physician, the doctor could see how his blood pressure was progressing, and he could make adjustments to his medications as needed.

Margarita had become indispensable. Este, now in kindergarten, was also going to a private school that was being paid for by the Gray family.

Mrs. Gray had won the election and was very busy in Congress. She spent very little time at home.

One Sunday afternoon, while Mr. Gray was playing golf, he fell to the ground. He couldn't speak or move the right side of his body. His friend, Dr. Stilson, who had been playing golf with him, examined him and realized that Mr. Gray was having a stroke, a cerebral vascular accident, or CVA. They immediately called 911 for an ambulance. His golfing friends placed Mr. Gray on the golf cart, and by the time they got to the parking lot, the ambulance was arriving. The paramedics took Mr. Gray to the nearby trauma center that was a neuro receiving center as well. The interventional radiologist placed a catheter into the artery causing the blockage to the circulation into Mr. Gray's brain. Using some contrast medication, he was able to find the clot and restore the circulation to the brain; however, much damage had already been done.

Brain cells are easily injured, and the brain cells frequently die from lack of circulation of blood needed for the normal function in the brain. The sooner the circulation returns to the injured cells, the better chance that the injured portion of the brain will be able to recover from the lack of circulation. Time can only tell how injured Mr. Gray's brain was and if he was going to recover at all. Sometimes, some of the functions return faster than others, depending on how badly that portion of the brain is injured.

After the intervention, Mr. Gray was immediately taken to the intensive care unit. He remained there for weeks; eventually, he was moved to a regular hospital room to recuperate. When his condition stabilized, he was sent home to continue to recuperate; that way he could be with his family. At home, he had twenty-four-hour nursing care that would turn him over every couple of hours. His neurologist came to see him every day. He also had daily physical therapy that would move his joints. He would cry every day. It was so sad to see him. It was hard for his children to be around him. He was helpless to communicate; he couldn't say a word, and he could not move. The nurse helped him with all his bodily functions. He had a Foley catheter to urinate. It seemed hopeless. Margarita would come every day to hold his hand and to sing for him. She would wash his face and, in her own loving, gentle way, would kiss him on the forehead. Months passed, and Mr. Gray began to improve. Margarita, who would massage his legs every day, began to nice a slight movement in Mr. Gray's right toes. With time, he began to move his right leg and started having bladder and stool functions, so he did not have to have the Foley catheter anymore. They bought him a wheelchair, and Margarita would take him out to the nearby park where he could listen to the birds and see the flowers and the trees and experience some fresh air. His improvements became more evident, and soon, he was able to stand; however, he made little progress with his speech. He started walking with much difficulty. Margarita would help him walk. He was having daily speech therapy. This, too, finally started to improve, and as the months went by, Mr. Gray began to normalize and, occasionally, was able to go to his office for a couple hours.

The Gray children were now going to college. Este was finishing the sixth grade in her elementary school. Mr. Gray was almost back to his normal activities. Margarita wanted to get a job to contribute to the care of Este.

Mr. Gray had a childhood friend who was a director in a Broadway play. He got Margarita a job cleaning the performers' rooms and helping with whatever they needed or wanted. She was a go-for girl. She would make coffee for them, get them doughnuts, sandwiches, cigarettes, or she would go to the post office for them or do last-minute ironing. She would do whatever they asked. Soon, she was very well liked and loved by all of members of the play. Again, she was indispensable.

Margarita would watch with much interest and enthusiasm while they practiced for the play. She would go to her room and practice the dances and the lines of the star of the play, Brenda. Margarita had all the lines memorized. Sometimes, going down the halls of the studio, she would sing the songs of the play and do some of the dances. She was a natural singer and dancer.

The play was about a young executive, multimillionaire, a very handsome man that travels to Rio de Janeiro on business. He sees this incredibly beautiful young girl that has finished cleaning his room at the Windsor Marapendi hotel. He happens to arrive as she is leaving the room, and is about to close the door. She says to him with a big, beautiful smile that lights up the room: "Have a nice day, sir." He is immediately taken by her poise, her charm, and beauty. He says to her: "Wait a minute. Would you like to have dinner with me tonight?" She responds: "It is against the hotel rules for me to get involved with the guest." She is closing the door as she goes out when one of her co-workers asks her, "Are you going with us to the Minina Club tonight?" She replies, "Of course, I would not miss it for the world." She shuts the door. The young executive, whose name is Henry, is very attracted to the young Brazilian girl, Aline. He thinks he is falling in love with her. He heard Alina say that she was going to the Minina Club. Aline lives in the Favela, the poor side of town. Henry decides he is going to conquer her. That night, he shows up at the Minina Club with a big bouquet of red roses. Aline is not interested. Henry begins to fall in love with Aline. He sees her dancing the samba. She is very beautiful and graceful and full of personality. He watches her all night, then decides to talk to her. He tells her that he has fallen in love with her, and he wants to marry her. He wants to give her everything. He wants to take her to Beverly Hills, where she can live in a mansion and have everything she wants. She replies, "I would never marry for money," she said. "I would only marry for love." The young executive tells her that he is willing to give up all of his money and fortune and would be willing to live with her in the Favela to show his love for her. She eventually falls in love with him, and they live happily ever after.

Brenda had to take several months of training so that she could have the Latin accent for the play. One day, Brenda, the star of the play, had fallen going down the stairs after having a few drinks and, unfortunately, broke her lower leg. This was a great setback for the play. The director was desperate; he could not find anyone to fit in with such short notice. He had to find a solution. The director had seen Margarita dancing and singing down the hall. He got the idea to try Margarita and see if she could fit into Brenda's role in the play. Margarita was fantastic on her first try. She had the natural Latin accent that the director was looking for. The director thought that she was a born actress. Margarita had her first try in a famous Broadway play called The Day We Met. The director told Margarita that she needed to change her name and have a stage name for her acting career. He suggested Margelina for her new name as an actress.

⸺⸺⸻❖⸻⸺⸺

Years back, Britana had her baby boy, Hernan. He was truly beautiful, and Antonio fell in love with him the minute his baby was born. He called him Herny.

It is a very difficult and confusing experience for a baby to be born in a royal family.

With a newborn baby there is a thing called "bonding." Bonding is a process in which the baby bonds with his mother who takes care of the baby with love and tenderness. She gives him her breastmilk. The baby gets used to the mother's heartbeat. He feels protected and knows she will always take care of him. He knows that she will always keep him safe and warm and will always be there for him. That bond begins to form that creates that sense of ownership between them that will last a lifetime. That is the bonding process.

The baby that is born to a royal family, his world is very confusing. The baby does not know who the parents are. Though the babies have the best material things, the best cribs, the best sheets, the best diapers and nannies, the heartbeat changes, and they are confused. They don't know with whom they should bond.

The royal babies have the house servants do it all. The babies go from hand to hand. Frequently, these royal parents would hire what they called the "lactating nurse." These women may have babies of their own or may have older children. They come and give the royal babies "la teta" (breastmilk). This confuses royal babies, who have servants do it all; they often have little contact with their mother.

The lactating nurses were very common, and they did not necessarily have to have a new baby.

These lactating women had their babies and started lactating years before and sold their milk to the royal families, having the royal babies sucking up the lactating nurse's milk.

The usual scenario may be that the mother of the royal baby frequently is too busy and has other social things to entertain her. Occasionally, the mother may ask for the baby. "Come to mommy," she may say. Frequently, the baby cries and is confused; the mother may then say, "I am your mommy." If the baby keeps crying, she may give orders to take the baby away. The mother almost always is more interested in herself and her social world than her baby.

These lactating nurses often lasted years. If the mammary glands are being stimulated, they keep producing milk. It was common that a lactating nurse could give of her milk to several children in the family.

Antonio was a fantastic father. He did not want the house servants around his son. He made Britana give his son Herny "la teta," the mother's breastmilk. Britana and Antonio were good parents to Herny. Antonio had to make Britana cancel many social events because he wanted her to be there to give his son "la teta" and her attention.

As the years passed, it was obvious that Herny was a special and gifted child. He was looked at by the royal families as the golden boy. He had golden blond hair. Herny made friends wherever he went. He spent much time with his father. They adored each other.

When Herny was four years old, Herny's parents decided they would let him attend a nursery school for the royals and the rich and famous. Antonio always picked up his son from school.

Herny would come home excited and full of enthusiasm. He wanted to share with his father and mother about the events of his day. His parents gave him much attention, and he seemed to mature much faster than the other children.

Antonio noticed that his son had exceptional physical and mental abilities, and he tried to develop his obvious gift for sports. Herny ran much faster than other kids his age. He was the star of his soccer team. His parents also had him playing tennis. Herny loved sports. It was his expression of life. His parents organized his life so that he could have his formal schooling done at home, one on one with his teachers. His father had always loved sports and loved to participate when he could. Antonio would get up early every morning and go for his five-kilometer run. That was his daily routine.

This was the beginning of Margelina's rolep in show business. She not only preformed on Broadway plays but soon began to have many opportunities in Hollywood and became a famous movie star. She moved to Hollywood and said goodbye to the kind Gray family that had given her a hand and opportunity that permitted her to start a new life. She had many opportunities to be romantically involved with influential, talented, and handsome and powerful men, but she always chose to stay behind and put her attention on her daughter Este.

Margarita couldn't get Antonio out of her mind. She remembered how they played when they were children and how they had pledged their love for each other. She wished she had the pendent he had given her, "his heart for her to keep."

Antonio's mother began to have symptoms of Alzheimer's disease. She started forgetting the names of people and things. She was very ashamed of this and often kept to herself. She frequently got lost and denied she was lost. She became more aggressive and sometimes became violent.

There are several kinds of Alzheimer's disease. Some people have the violent kind, in which the patient is unkind to family, friends, and caretakers to the point of being physically violent to them. This was the kind of Alzheimer's disease that Mrs. Del Rey had. This disease is a gradual deterioration of the brain that eventually leads to death. It can come at middle age or later in life.

It often starts with losing their social skills. They don't want to be with their friends and relatives because they forget names and things, and they are ashamed of this. Then comes the disorientation and loss of memory. They lose the ability to recognize their family and friends and caretakers and often get lost. Then comes the loss of daily bodily functions, where they defecate and urinate without any control and at any moment. They then lose their appetite and their motor skills, being unable to walk. And as the brain continues to deteriorate, they lose their respiratory and cardiac functions, leading to death. This, of course, can take years, or it can move more rapidly.

⟶⟶⟶◆⟵⟵⟵

The monarchy was being challenged in Spain by Franco. Many of the royal families were forced to abandon their homes and their way of life, and of course, their money and property were taken away from them. Some families frequently took refuge in nearby European countries; sometimes they were forced to live their lives as "commoners."

Antonio's brother, Eduardo, had chosen to flee to Portugal where his wife had relatives. Antonio chose to stay home and take care of his ailing mother and ill wife. Since he could no longer live in the castle, he decided to move into the old house where Margarita's family had lived. He camouflaged himself so that they would think he was one of the workers.

Britana, because of the inbreeding in her family, contracted a genetic disorder that had to come from both sides of the family via recessive genes that came from her mother and father. She had a condition known as retinitis pigmentosa. This is a condition that can start at a fairly early age or later in life. Often in the late twenties or early thirties. At first, the patients do not recognize the problem, and they live in denial.

Normally, the retina picks up the images that we look at. It works like a mirror. It sends these images to the brain via the optic nerve, then the brain responds with the appropriate action. With Retinitis Pigmentosa, the retina begins to have dark pigment that forms around the edges of the retina, making that part of the retina unable to capture the images. This makes the person gradually lose their peripheral vision. As the condition progresses and the pigment involves more of the retina, the persons begin to lose more and more of their peripheral vision. They start having tunnel vision. Eventually, they end up looking through a tiny little hole in the retina, before they go totally blind. Because they lose the ability to see their periphery, they often have many accidents. This happened to Britana, as she got hit by a car in an unfortunate fatal accident. Britana had been kind to Antonio. Though he never was able to fall in love with her, they were able to have a congenial respectful and peaceful marriage. Antonio was sad to see Britana go; after all, she was the mother of his beloved son, Herny. Antonio was left to care for Herny with the help of Pablo. Antonio had been taken care of Britana for several years before she had this sad and unfortunate accident.

Antonio also has to care for his mother alone, since his father had been murdered and found dead some years back, with several shots in his head and body.

Mr. Del Rey, Julio, had started a love relationship with the widow of Felipe, Regina. Felipe was the man that had died during the duel with Julio, when Julio was just twenty years old. Sometime after the duel, Julio had gone to see Regina to give her his condolences since he felt bad about having killed her husband. The two of them became friends and, eventually, became lovers.

It was very difficult for Regina to have sexual relations with Julio. She remembered what a painful experience it had been for her, and she wanted nothing to do with sex. Felipe had been so forceful and unkind, this caused her to be unable to lubricate, and sex hurt her and irritated her every time she had sex with Felipe.

Julio, with his gentleness and kindness and love and tenderness, had thought Regina how to enjoy making love. She lubricated just fine, and she always looked forward to his visit.

Back then, when anyone had a lover, everyone knew about it. The house servants were always taking care of the guest, and soon, everyone knew. The gossip moved faster than the deed. It was very common in those days to have a lover.

Every day, Julio would go on his horse to visit his love, Regina. He thought riding his horse was more romantic. He would spend the day with her and then ride home in the late afternoon. Julio and Regina had a very especial relationship, and they loved being together. They took long walks together and made love in the fields, amongst the flowers. Julio would take her on his horse, and they would go to the nearby river and go for a swim naked and spend the afternoon together.

Felipe, who was a very wealthy man, when he was confronted with the slight possibility that he would be killed during the duel, had decided to put his financial business in order. He made a will leaving Regina the castle that they lived in. He also left her a large amount of money so that she could continue to live in the same style she had been living when she lived with Felipe. He left the rest of his holdings to his two sons, Marco and Ramon.

Unfortunately, Julio and Regina had a very difficult and serious problem. The two sons of Felipe, now adults, decided to live in the mansion where Regina lived. They did this on purpose to make Regina's life impossible to tolerate. They tried to disrupt her life any way they could. They were especially upset that she had found a relationship with the man that had killed their father. This made for a very uncomfortable situation for poor Regina. Julio, who did not seem to have any fear from them, always told Regina to just ignore them.

When Felipe died, of course, Regina, being his widow, wore black for a couple years as was the custom in Spain. She tried to act like a grieving widow. Inside of her head, she was very glad that Felipe had died. He was so unkind and abusive to her. She was incarcerated in this relationship without any chance of getting out. She often would cry and felt helpless until Felipe died. After he died, she was alone for three years before she finally permitted someone who was kind, understanding, loving, and never forceful to capture her heart and body. Since then, she couldn't wait to see Julio every day.

When Felipe died, Felipe's mother, Maria, had asked her grandsons Marco and Ramon to come and live with her and her husband. They chose to stay with Regina and continued to live in the castle they had always known since they were born. Regina was just a few years older than them, and she agreed to let them stay. As they continued to grow and Regina developed the relationship with Julio, the war began, and between the two of them, they had vowed to make her life impossible, and as the time went on, they talked about revenge.

Regina was so in love with Julio, she would have lunch made and placed in a basket, and she would wait for him under the shade of the old oak tree. She would place a tablecloth on the ground, and they would have lunch together. After lunch, Julio would lie his head on her lap, and they would dream about their plans for the future.

Andrea was totally incoherent by now, and Julio and Regina talked about the day they could live together. Julio was only six years older than Regina, and many years had passed in their relationship that had started before Andrea became ill.

The anniversary of Felipe's death was coming up. Marco and Ramon begin to plan how they were going to kill Regina and Julio. Several years had passed, and they both talked about how they needed to kill them. Neither one of them had the courage to do it. They had tried years before to poison them with rat poison when Julio had stayed for lunch one day. Fortunately, Regina told Julio: "It is a beautiful day to eat inside. What do you think if we have some sandwiches made, and we spend the afternoon at the river? I can ask the cook to make them; that way, we can go for a swim." Julio liked the idea, and they went to the nearby river. Unfortunately, one of the house servants had eaten the food that had been poisoned and died of "unexplainable causes."

The boys decided they would try something else. Now that they were older, they decided they needed to act. Like their father, they liked to go into town to the red district to be with the prostitutes. The owner of the whorehouse was this obese, dishonorable drunk they called Sapo. Last week, Sapo and Marco had been drinking together, and Marco told Sapo about how he wanted to kill Julio and Regina. He asked Sapo if he would do it if they paid him ten thousand pesetas. Sapo agreed to do it. Marco told him that he wanted them dead on the anniversary of their father's death.

One Tuesday evening, Julio did not come home. His horse had come home without him. Antonio went looking for his father the next day, only to find his father and Regina dead on the ground. They both had several bullet holes in the head and torso.

These were tough times for Antonio, who loved his father dearly, and now was left to take care of his ailing mother alone.

Soon after that, his own family had come apart, having to flee as the Spaniards were no longer going to accept these wealthy royal families that were taking away the money that could go into the politicians' pockets.

The Del Rey family had this wooden cedar chess that was always locked. This was where the family kept their gold coins and precious jewelry. They also kept large amounts of money in the Geneva banks. When Eduardo left for Portugal, Antonio and Eduardo divided the family fortune.

Eduardo asked his brother if they could arrange it so that his daughter Marina could marry Antonio's son Herny. Antonio did not agree. He did not want any part of this proposal. He told his brother that even though it was the way things had always been done in their family for generations, he wanted his son to be the first one in their family to make his own decision about who he was going to marry.

Antonio told his brother, "Our family is coming apart, and it is a good time that we learn to blend in and live our lives in a different way than we were used to. We will never again live in the same way we lived before." They hugged each other. They were both very sad to have lost both of their parents, but life must go on. "We must find a new way to live."

When many of these royal families had to flee, frequently, some of the house servants were loyal to their masters and helped get their masters and their fortune out of Spain. They continued serving their master wherever they went; after all, they had served them for decades. It was the only life they knew. They had nowhere else to go. Pablo decided to stay with Antonio.

Antonio couldn't stop dreaming about Margarita. He remembered the first time he saw her when he was just a young boy, as she sang and danced in front of her family's porch. He remembered the times they played together, when he would yell "Margarita" and she would run out to play with him. He remembered when he went away to college, and he had given her the pendent and had kissed her for the first and only time. He remembered when he saw her for the last time, when she was bleeding down her leg and he had found the pendent that he had given her full of blood on top of the bed. He kept the pendent with him all the time. He looked at it every night before he went to sleep. He remembered what a sad day it had been for him, how he had to kill his childhood friend because he had torn his heart and soul, and now, he couldn't find the one person he had loved since childhood.

⸺⸺⸻❖⸻⸺⸺

Margelina became rich and famous. She became the most famous movie star in Hollywood. She remained single. At times, she thought she wants to go back and see the mansion where she grew up and had developed this great love for Antonio since they were children. She wished she had the pendent he had given her, his heart for her to keep. She remembered the brutal experience that had led to their separation. She remembered how Britana had been pregnant with Antonio's child. She remembered the bloody sheet she had seen after Antonio had spent the first night with Britana. She thought the only children that Antonio would ever have would be with her. She remembered how, when they were children, she really believed in her heart that she was going to live all her life with Antonio as they had dreamt. They would have a home and a family together. These were sad memories and unrealized dreams.

Though Margarita had become rich and famous and had received many awards for her performances, she felt unfulfilled and wanted to do something more with her life. She wanted to do something more meaningful. She had lost interest in her acting career. She wanted to find something that would make her feel not famous but something gratifying and fulfilling in her life. Something that would make her proud of herself. She had so much in her life, and she wanted to change the course of her life. She decided she wanted to be a psychologist. She enrolled at UCLA to begin her new studies to be a psychologist.

Her daughter Este was now attending Hollywood High. She tried out for the cheerleading squad and did very well. Like her mother, she was a natural dancer and had a very likeable personality. She was also very good looking and had a graceful way about her, as well as a fantastic figure. Her mother was very proud of her. Este was also accepted to the honors program at the high school. Aside from being the prettiest and the best dancer in the cheerleading squad, she is also a very good student. Margarita frequently accompanied her to the Friday night football games at Hollywood High.

Padre Francisco was kneeling again next to David's bed, saying his daily prayers, holding David's hand as he always does. He suddenly felt a slight movement in David's hand. He said to David: "If you can hear me, squeeze my hand." To his surprise, David squeezed Padre Francisco's hand. He ran to the church where he found Nelly, and he said: "It's a miracle! It's a miracle! It's a miracle!" he shouts. "I told you God had a plan for David. I know he is going to wake up."

The next day, David's eyes were open, but he couldn't move. With physical therapy and David's great desire to survive and walk and talk, David began to normalize.

Padre Francisco took him into the monastery, and David began his studies at the seminary to become a Catholic priest.

Antonio's mother had passed away some time back, before Eduardo left for Portugal. She died of a heart attack and Alzheimer's disease. Now that his wife and mother were gone, he only had Herny to worry about.

Antonio had great interest in computers. At that time, computers took a lot of space, sometimes taking the space of a small room. Most people did not understand much about computers. They were mostly used by the military and very sophisticated business. There were not many opportunities in Spain in the computer industry. After investigating, Antonio discovered that his best opportunity in the computer industry was at the University of California Berkley. This University offered a PhD in computer science. Antonio also discovered that the US government had been pouring millions of dollars into the University of California

Berkley military computer research center. Antonio decided to move to Berkley.

When the royal families were dismantled, Pablo decided to stay with Antonio. Antonio was his whole life. When Antonio moved to Berkley, he took Pablo with him. Pablo now worried about Herny.

While Herny was attending Berkeley High School, his father was attending the University of California at Berkley. Herny, aside from being a good student, he was an exceptional athlete, and soon contributed to the high school athletic program wherever he could. The high school football coach noticed him right away. He was the fastest runner in the whole school, and he had a lot of discipline at the gym trying to improve himself. The football coach thought he could train him to be his next quarterback for the following year when Herny would be a sophomore, or maybe a junior, depending how his current quarterback was preforming. Since Herny was a young child, he had been a fantastic athlete. He had played soccer most of his life, but when he came to live in the US, he developed a passion for college football and the NFL. During his High School sophomore year, he began to pay attention to how the quarterback handled the ball and coordinated the plays. He continued to work out hard at the gym to improve his strength, speed, and muscle bulk. He was six feet, four inches tall. He was really a fantastic athlete, but more, he had the discipline to be the best.

In the middle of the football season of his sophomore year, the first-string quarterback's family moved to Chicago, and the coach decided to try out Herny. He did well right away and continued to improve as time went by. He got more experience, and his performance improved drastically. Berkley High had a winning season. They had found their quarterback.

Every football season, he continued to improve himself. When Herny was a senior, he was rated as the number one high school quarterback in the nation. The different universities sent their scouts and recruiters to talk to him and his dad to offer them their best deal. They were courting him to get him to play football at their university. Herny decided to play for his favorite college football team, the Ohio State Buckeyes. This was his favorite college football team since he started watching college football. He felt bad that he would be so far from his dad. Herny and his dad had a very close and loving relationship, and his father was very proud of him.

Antonio got his PhD in computer science. He started working in the computer research lab for the US government in Berkley. He invented a device for the military that was small and fit in the ear. The device was waterproof, and with this device, the soldiers could communicate with the other members in their military unit. It coordinated with the new secret GPS system that had been recently invented for the military. This gave perfect orientation all the time.

Americans were involved in one of the most unpopular and, at that time, the longest war in the history of the United States, The Viet Nam War. Most Americans could not understand why they were involved in this war that was killing so many of their young men for an unknown cause. It was a time when the draft was implemented, and at that time, when the boys turned into men at the age of eighteen, the law stipulated that they had to register for the draft at the draft board or go to jail. If they were good students in college, they were able to apply for a student deferment. They still had to register, but if they were good students, they were eligible for a student deferment.

Young men were being forced to give their lives in this war that did not threaten our nation and did not have the interest of our country. There was a lot of discord and demonstrations everywhere, especially in Northern California and in Berkley where much of the hippie community resided. There were forceful demonstrations against the war. They had riots and burned buildings, and they would burn their draft cards to show their disconformity and defiance against the war.

The device that Antonio had invented coordinated with a translating device that translated the Vietnamese language to the English language and was also able to, when properly programed, decipher the Vietcong scripted communications that had been deciphered by the US military. It was a secret device used only by the military, and only by Special Forces.

Antonio was strong and tall. He ran five kilometers every morning and went to the gym every day. He had designed this device especially for a very unique and well-trained group of soldiers. This was a special secret unit of military men that were involved in search and rescue, code name "secure." They were trained by the military for this specific duty. They were in the reserve branch of the military. Most had their own civilian jobs but had to maintain an outstanding physical condition. They got together periodically for training exercises to maintain their coordination as a group. There were only twenty of them, and they had to be ready at a moment's notice to go where ever they were needed and do their job they were trained to do, and come home. Antonio was in charge of this unit.

⚜

Margarita also finished her PhD in psychology. She started a project to help returning veterans. She developed a foundation called The Veteran's Home. This helped the veterans that came home with post-traumatic stress disorder and other physical and emotional and mental problems. She wanted to help the injured veterans that came home with missing limbs, broken bones, broken spirits, and broken hearts. They lacked social skills that were taken from them in a cruel and violent war. She wanted to help them improve their self-esteem. She involved other psychologists that were specialized in this unfortunate problem of post-traumatic stress disorder as well as physicians, physical and occupational therapists. Psychologists that were experts in family group therapy. She built a large place where they could meet and share their stories. Social areas where the families could be together, where they could get to know each other, and share with other military families how they are coping with the disabilities the soldiers are bringing home. Their husbands that left for war were not the same people that came home. Now they had to learn to live with this stranger, the husband and the father of their children, who had come home from this cruel war.

She built a large kitchen and a dining area where they could eat their favorite foods. She included a pharmacy and had a full-time pharmacist. She had physical and occupational and emotional therapy clinics. She had a rehab center for the returning vets with drug addiction. There was a department of housing that was responsible for finding veterans a comfortable place to live with their families and their disabilities. She built a gymnasium where the children could play and the veterans could have some physical activity.

Many of the Hollywood stars and other celebrities were impressed with Margelina's project and were more than willing to contribute to her foundation.

Este has finished high school, and she has decided to go to college nearby so she wouldn't be far from her mother. She decided to attend USC, the University of Southern California.

Margelina was admired not only by her peers in Hollywood but also by the American people, the military, and, of course, the veterans.

David become a priest and was sent to the Philippines as a missionary. There, he was in charge of an Old Catholic Mission. Many years before he arrived, a Spanish-style church had been built by the Spaniards who started the mission. It has a high wooden ceiling and stained-glass windows, which were a true work of art. It was a very beautiful church. It was built by the Spaniards more than a hundred years before. And it was built right in the corner of the plaza. They went through great lengths, more than a hundred years before, to make this beautiful church in this little village. Aside from the church, the mission has a big chunk of land in the back with fruit trees and vines. There were always chickens and ducks running around and, of course, the pigs and the mud. When Padre David, as they called him (the Spaniards colonized the Philippines for decades, and many Spanish terms and customs linger on, and the Catholic Church has had a special relationship with the Philippines), discovered that there had been corruption in the church. He began to change all of that. The money that came to the church that previously had no accountability was now being used to build schools. They started cooking every day lots of food to feed the poor in this small village. Within the compounds of the church property, Padre David, over the years, had built a school, had also built an orphanage, and a place to provide food, education, shelter, and medical and emotional care for the less fortunate. This, of course, was financed in a large part by donations of the Catholic Church.

Padre David was adored by everyone. He would listen to the families' problems and helped them fix them. He gave them hope; he taught them respect for one and other. He was one of the family. Whatever problem they might be having, like problems with the family or money problems, or problems with drugs, problems with friends or pregnancies, he always helped them fix them. He was always there for them. He, aside from being their spiritual leader, was also the psychologist, a friend, a "curandero," as they sometimes called him. (He delivered most of the kids in town.) The parents always name him "the padrino." In reality, the village couldn't function without his loving kindness and devotion. His gift he had for the church was to spread love and hope and kindness. It was obvious that he was a man of God and he loved what he did.

Viet Nam was close by, and the Vietcong were using the Philippines for training purposes. They were a criminal organization, killing anyone who would oppose them. Unfortunately, they took over the Catholic mission and imprisoned the priest and his staff. They killed anyone who got in the way. Padre David and his staff were forced to make food for the soldiers who raped the women and abused the children.

⟶ ⟫⟩❖⟨⟪ ⟵

One morning, when Margelina was in her office as usual, working on her project, her secretary knocked on her door and said: "There is a general here to see you."

"Ask him to come in," said Margelina. When he came through the door, there was a tall, confident, three-starred army general that had come to see her.

Margelina asked him to sit down. Her secretary asked the general if she could offer him something to drink. The general said, "No, thank you." The general said: "I'll get to the point. I know you are the most beautiful and talented and most popular entertainer that we as Americans are lucky to have. You are a great example of someone that really loves her country, and we are very thankful for what you do with our veterans. That is why I venture to come and talk to you."

The General then asked Margelina if she was willing to go to Viet Nam to entertain the American troops. Margelina, years before, had become an American citizen, and she loved being an American. She told the general that it would be a privilege and an honor to serve her country. The general told Margelina that someone from the military would be contacting her to work out the details.

Margarita had a crew of people that would have to go with her. Her personal manager that would arrange the time and place where she would perform and also made sure she got enough rest. Also, the person that helped her with her makeup and her hair. The person that would worry about her food (she was a vegetarian) and where she will stay, and her musicians, just a few, that would accompany her singing and dancing. It was a group reduced to only twelve people.

The arrangements were made, and Margelina and her group are on their way to Viet Nam. Upon her arrival, she was given a warm welcome and taken to the place where she would stay for the first night, along with her crew.

It was monsoon season in Viet Nam, and there was water everywhere. The rain seemed to come down in buckets, and it never stopped. Margelina would perform for a different group of soldiers each night for ten days, then she would fly home. She was moved from place to place, preforming for different groups of the armed forces.

One night, as they were being transported to perform for a group of Marine soldiers, they were ambushed on route by the Vietcong, and Margelina and her group were taken hostage to an unknown destination.

On arrival to Vietnam, Margelina's group had been given these tall boots that had an electronic chip that was embedded inside the boots; this way, they could track them in case of any unforeseen problem. Because of the large amounts of water and mud, the boots were waterproof and tall, up to the knee. This gave them protection from the mud that was everywhere.

Fortunately, Antonio's search and rescue unit was in the Philippines for some night training exercises during the monsoon season. Antonio and his search and rescue unit were called and immediately transported to nearby Vietnam. On route, they studied the best way to approach the situation. They put their night gear on and took their underwater equipment. On arrival, they were able to intercept their communication and break into their scripted messages. Soon, they knew exactly where they are keeping Margelina and her group.

Water was six inches deep in most places. There was a waterway that ran along the side of most of the country and was near the military base where they were keeping Margelina and her group. Antonio and his unit were transported by helicopter, and they were dropped near the waterway.

The waterway was at least ten feet deep and about fifty yards wide. They were dropped off five miles from the base where they were keeping Margelina and her crew. They dropped them there, so they would not be noticed upon arrival. Antonio and his unit were carrying explosives, night-vision equipment, and aside from their ear device, they also had other communication equipment to communicate with the American base nearby. They had their waterproof backpacks where they kept it all. The men entered the water way, swimming on their back, permitting only their nose to be out of the water so they could breathe and not be detected. They had trained for this kind of mission. The waterway was moving rapidly; this made it easy for them to reach their destination. They were used to maneuvers at night without being detected. The GPS was giving them the exact location of where they need to attack. When they arrived, it is 3 a.m.; all was quiet. The Vietnamese have placed Margelina and her group outside, in the middle of their compound, in the deep mud and severe rain. They were incarcerated by a surrounding chain-link fence, and there were Vietcong soldiers guarding them.

The Vietcong have gotten some communication by an informant. They informed them that a helicopter had landed near the waterway and had dropped off several soldiers wearing black fatigues. They were going down the waterway. As a result of the information, last minute, the Vietcong decided to take out Margelina and her crew and transport them to the compound in the Philippines, where the Catholic mission exists. The Viet Cong had Margelina's crew take off all of their clothing and boots and had given them blankets to cover themselves. They discovered the electronic chips inside the boots and moved the boots to the center of their compound so that the Americans would think the crew was there. The Vietcong prepared themselves so that when the Americans arrived to get them, they would ambush them and finish them off.

When Margelina and her group arrived in the Philippines, they were given uniforms and were told to stay quiet. They take them all into the church. A Viet Cong officer came into the church with some other officers; he appeared to be in command. He asked, "Who is in charge here?"

Padre David stood up and said, "I am."

The Viet Cong officer asked him to come up.

He then took his knife and slit Padre David's throat and cuts off his head completely. Blood was pumping everywhere. He took the amputated head by the hair. The blood was pooling on the floor. He then said, "This is what will happen to you if you try to escape or make any noise or go against our orders."

Everyone was terrified. There was total silence. The officer looked around the church, then he turn around and went out the door.

They all gathered in the center of the church, trying not to let their crying be heard. There was desperation in all of their faces. There was a sense of hopelessness. There was total silence.

Meanwhile, when Antonio and his men arrived at the Viet Cong base, they observed the situation from afar for a period of time. They knew, however, that they had to make their move before the sun came up.

They noticed with the GPS that the signal from the boots was static, and there was not the slightest bit of movement. They thought perhaps they had killed them all and that was the reason why there was no movement. This tipped them off that something was not right. Antonio and his men noticed that the base was heavily guarded, and it was obvious that they were waiting for them, so they pulled back about a half a mile. Antonio was able to climb an electrical power tower about a half a mile away, and with his powerful telescopic lens with night vision, he could see that they have piled the boots in the center of the compound. Antonio and his men mined the road to the entrance of the compound without being detected. This was their specialty, working at night without being detected. They retreated.

They walked all the early morning hours back to the American base where they rested for a couple hours. Antonio and his men began looking for other alternatives.

They monitored Vietcong communications, but there was total silence. Antonio knew that if they were going to find them alive, they had to find them soon. The American military base got a tip from the Catholic Church.

The Catholics had asked the Americans to help them get their missionaries out of the Philippines some time back. The American generals had been considering a raid on the Catholic mission but were afraid of hurting civilians.

Early in the morning, they received new information. Someone reported to the Catholic Church in the Philippines that they have seen some prisoners, including several women, brought to the Catholic mission. They locked them up in the church.

Antonio and his men begin to study the maps of the Catholic compound and started making plans to attack, being careful to avoid civilian casualties. Antonio's group were now wearing civilian clothing so they would not be detected. They were flown in a civilian plane to the Manila airport so they would not cause any suspicion. Four vans in different locations were waiting at the airport to pick them up. They were taken to a large house, not too far from the mission. There, they had all the equipment they would need to make their move.

The Catholic mission that the Vietcong were using as a base in the Philippines was supposed be a secret, but of course, the Americans knew all about it. The Vietcong did everything they could to keep it a secret. They tortured and killed several of the mission's staff to intimidate and threatened the rest. If they said anything to expose them, they would kill their families and the rest of the group. The Vietcong have the Catholic mission well-fortified.

All of the mission's staff lived in total fear and desperation every day. There was no hope. They kept their heads down. They cooked for them and washed their clothing, trying to make everyone think like all is normal. They didn't want to cause any problems.

Though the Catholic Church knew that their mission had been invaded by the Vietcong, they felt impotent; they wanted no violence, but they were desperate to get their people out without further violence.

Antonio and his men waited for nightfall. They were experts at maneuvering at night. On arrival, after looking around from a far and getting a feel for the area, they rested all afternoon. At midnight, they put their plan in motion.

Killing was very difficult for Antonio and his men, especially when they had to use a knife and slit the throat of the soldiers guarding the compound, but this was their mission, and they have been trained for this. They know they have to save the lives of the Americans being held.

They went into the mission and started the assault. After taking the guards outside, they were very careful to make sure that there was total silence, and they had taken out all of them. They then moved to take out the guards around the church. One by one, they slit their throats and take them all out. Most of the guards were asleep. In total silence, they evacuated all of the hostages from the Church and moved them to a safe area down the street below. They now had to fight the soldiers in the compound so that a helicopter could land and take out the hostages. They called for the helicopter. Then began to throw grenades where the soldiers were sleeping. Gunfire erupted, and there was a horrific fight. The first helicopter landed and was able to evacuate the hostages that were waiting outside the compound, about a half mile down the street. The fight continued, and finally, the gunfire stopped. Slowly and one by one, they began to inspect all of the buildings and the houses in the compound, occasionally finding some soldiers that were giving up.

Antonio's job was over, and he began to gather his men. He called for the second helicopter. Several of his men were injured, none seriously. They couldn't find Jim, Antonio's best friend. Suddenly, a single gunshot was heard. When they found Jim, he was dead; he had taken a bullet through his head. A second gunshot was heard as the second helicopter arrived. Antonio spotted the sniper on the roof and rapidly took him out with a single shot. All of them moved rapidly into the helicopter. Antonio went back to pick up his best friend's body. They were all in the helicopter, and as Antonio and his men were pulling Jim's body into the helicopter, they came into hostile fire again. Antonio was always the last one into the helicopter, and he always said, "Leave no men behind." Unfortunately, as Antonio was boarding and the helicopter was pulling out, Antonio took a bullet to the chest.

Margelina and her group arrive at the US base. They were placed immediately in a military plane bound for LA. Margelina and her crew arrived in LA safely.

Margelina, who has been helping the veterans that came home injured physically and emotionally because of the violence of war, became a stronger advocate against the war. She realized firsthand how young American men were being sacrificed, losing their lives and limbs, many of them coming home disabled, confused, and unable to have a normal life. Others, unfortunately, arrived in a box, causing much sadness to their family and their friends. Margelina started a campaign against President Johnson and the war effort.

Antonio's injury through his right chest had caused a pneumothorax, a collapsed lung. He was very fortunate it had not caused damage to any mayor vessels or airways. On his arrival, he was taken immediately to surgery at the base hospital.

Antonio, after the first medical intervention in Vietnam, had evolved positively, and his lung was almost fully inflated in a few days. He was transferred in a special medical plane to the Long Beach Veterans Hospital to recuperate from his injury. His son, who had been informed, was brought to the hospital to stay with his Dad, and he stayed with him until he was stable and they were able to send Antonio home.

Herny loved his father dearly. He had been his hero all his life. They have had a loving and admirable relationship since Herny could remember. His father was everything to him. Herny knew that his father was in the military in the reserves. Antonio's unit was top secret, so he had been unable to share with his son about his involvement in this unit.

Occasionally, Herny would see his father leave for a few days, and his father would always tell him that he was doing some military exercises with his unit. Antonio did not worry when he had to go because he knew he has Pablo who was always home to make sure Herny was okay.

After Herny left to go back to the university, Antonio's commanding officer, General Raymond Canon, came to visit Antonio. He told him that his unit was being dismantled and would be managed by the Marine Special Forces. He thanks Antonio for his bravery and his willingness to give all for his country. He told him that he would be receiving the Purple Heart medal. He also brings him a letter from the Catholic Church, addressed to Cornel Antonio Del Rey.

Antonio is brokenhearted that he has lost his best friend with a bullet through his head. He felt terrible that his friend Jim had arrived in a box. He felt bad that he would not even attend his funeral. He called Jim's wife, Peggy, and they both cried together on the phone. He couldn't get over it.

His unit had never lost a man before. They had injuries, some of them serious, but they all had been able to return home and preform their job. Antonio was happy that his unit was being dismantled. He thought he was getting too old, and he can't live through another experience like this, where he lost a man and there was so much killing. Now, he was finally able to share with his beloved son the truth about his military past.

Herny was back at the university. Football was his passion. In his sophomore year, he was made the first-string quarterback. As usual, he was very successful as a quarterback. He was a running quarterback for the Buckeyes and was very effective. He was tall and strong and a fast runner. He was admired everywhere he went on campus.

Este has joined the cheerleading squad at USC. She was strikingly beautiful, energetic, friendly, and a fantastic dancer; like Herny, she was very well liked on campus.

Usually the football coach did not like his football players getting involved with the cheerleaders, but it was very common and a very difficult thing to regulate. Every Friday after the game, especially when they had a victory, the Trojans of USC, would get together to celebrate.

Este and Herny had developed a romance that started in their freshmen year when the Ohio State Buckeyes first came to play against the USC Trojans, before Herny was a quarterback. The two football teams had a social event at USC. It was a social event for the players of the two teams to get to know each other and socialize. It was then that he met Este and sparked a romance that had blossomed over the years.

Herny had a fantastic college football experience at Ohio State. And now, in his final year, the USC Trojans were going to meet the Ohio State Buckeyes at the Rose Bowl in Pasadena on New Year's Day. This would be televised nationwide, and Herny was looking forward to this event.

Herny took every opportunity to see Este. He called her every day. He spent weeks during his summer vacations in LA with his love, Este. She was everything to him. Occasionally, he would fly in for the weekend. He had to see her. Este loved and admired him. He was her hero. Herny has decided that he would marry Este when he finished college. He would announce it to the world after the game he knew he had to win.

Margelina had invited all of the Trojans, as well as the Buckeyes, their parents, and the coaches to her home for a celebration after the game. Her house has been made to accommodate a large party. She had a big house in the Hollywood Hills with a large party room overlooking LA. The room opened up into a big backyard that had gazebos, a swimming pool, waterfalls, fountains, many trees, gardens, and beautiful flowers, all with a fabulous view of LA. They were celebrating a successful football season for USC and Ohio State. Este invited Herny to the party and asked him to bring his father because she wanted to meet him.

Herny invited his father to the party. The party would be at Margelina's house, he told him. Antonio had come out several times to see his son play college football when they were playing close by. He could see himself in him. "That's my boy," he always said.

Herny told his dad that he is in love with Margelina's daughter, Este, since the first time he saw her when they were freshmen. He told his dad that he was going to marry her when he finished college. Herny told his father that he was going to meet Este and her mother at the party.

Antonio remembered the name Margelina in connection with the mission in Vietnam and the Philippines. He was pleasantly surprised by what his son told him, and he was looking forward to finally meeting this famous movie star Margelina.

Antonio, after he left the hospital, went to Peggie's house to give her his condolences and to finally tell her the truth about their secret unit and their secret mission. He told her how Jim had been so brave and had stayed behind and waited for the men to get into the chopper. He had suddenly disappeared, only to find him dead, with a bullet through his head. He gave his life for his country. He couldn't believe he would never have another barbeque with Jim again. He told her that he had always been his closest friend. "We talked every day. We told each other everything. He was always a kind, loyal, and honorable friend to me. I know nothing will ever replace him. I will miss him every day."

"The commanding officer came by and told me that Jim will be receiving the Medal of Honor for his bravery and service to his country," Antonio said. "My life will be very difficult without him." He then said: "Peggy, if you or the kids need anything, please let me know." They hugged and cried together. "I will be the father to your children. I have always been a part of this family, and that will never change."

At USC, all of the students were getting pumped up for the Rose Bowl game. Rallies everywhere, posters all over. The coach doesn't want the football players going anywhere for New Year's Eve. He kept them all together; that way, no one was going to stay up late or have a few drinks. He wanted all of them to do their best, to work as a unit, so they could take on the Buckeyes.

The football game was a nail-biter. Though USC had a great defense, the offence was not so good, and USC couldn't hold the Buckeyes offence. USC scored, then the Buckeyes scored. USC got ahead, then the Buckeyes caught up. Finally, it all came down to a field goal kick by the Buckeyes. They needed a fifty-two yarder to win the game. The clock had stopped with two seconds remaining. The Buckeyes' kicker came on to the field to kick the ball. Just as the center was about to hike the ball, the Trojans called a timeout. A common strategy. The ball was kicked, the players didn't know about the time out, and the kicker went ahead and kicked the ball. It was short. Because of the timeout prior to the kick, they had to kick it again. This gave the Buckeyes a second chance. This time, the ball hit the crossbar and landed in for a Buckeyes victory. The whole country was watching the Rose Bowl game, and they were amazed by the underdogs', the Buckeyes', last minute victory. The crowed in Pasadena were all standing and cheering.

Suddenly Herny appears in the center of the field on national TV with a microphone. He yells out: "Can you hear me?"

"Yeeeees!"

He said: "If you can stay in your seats a little longer, I have something I want to share with you." He then asked his girlfriend, Este, if she could come to the field with him. She, of course, had her USC cheerleading uniform on. The guards helped her on to the field, and she stood next to him. He went down on one knee and went on to say: "Este, I have fallen in love with you from the moment I saw you. Since then, I have admired your kindness, your beauty, your grace, your love for life, and your respect for others." He had one of his hands hidden behind his back. He went on to say, "Este, will you marry me?" He brought his hand out from behind him and took out a box; he opened it. It was a beautiful diamond ring.

"Oh, my love," she said, "I can never live without you. You are my prince, my love, my admiration, and my destiny; it will be a great honor to marry you and love you for the rest of my life." He took the ring from the box and placed it on her left ring finger. She said, "This is the most beautiful ring I have ever seen." They both kissed, and the crowd went wild.

Antonio remembered that Herny had asked him for two thousand dollars some months back. Antonio asked him what he needed that money for, and Herny just said: "You will see." Now Antonio understood what the money was for, and he said to himself, that is money well spent. Antonio was very proud of his son and was really looking forward to meeting Este and her mother. He was very happy he left the video recorder on at the house so that he could always look back to this moment.

Antonio had not seen Margarita for twenty-two years and had no clue that, on this night, he would see her after all these years.

He arrived at the party early. Margelina was sitting on the couch in the next room. The door was open, and Antonio walked down the hall; he started looking at the pictures on the wall. He saw pictures of Margarita when she was young. He even saw a picture of himself as a young man that she had kept all these years. Antonio finally realized that Margelina is really Margarita. He took the pendent he always kept with him, and he snuck behind Margarita and slowly and softly started to place it around her neck. She looked down at the pendent, and she screamed, "Antonio!" She turned around and puts her arms around him. Antonio locked the pendent around Margarita's neck. He said: "It is my heart for you to keep".

Margarita said: "I have never given my heart to anyone; it has always been all yours." She took him to her office where the two of them could have a private moment, as the tears fell and they were able to express the love and admiration they had always had for each other. They were both crying and holding each other. They realized that nothing had changed; they still had that love and sense of ownership for one and other. She said: "I have always wondered if Herny Del Rey was related to you."

They began to talk; they had so much to catch up on. Antonio told her that Britana had lost her life in a car accident. He told her that he never gave her his heart. They, however, had a civil marriage. He told her how his mother had died also and how they had to escape from Spain. He told her about his mission in Vietnam and the Philippines to rescue her and her group. He said he was proud of her, how she had risked her life for her country, going to Vietnam for the soldiers. He told her that, sadly, his best friend Jim had been killed during the mission. Margarita couldn't believe that Antonio had been one of the men that saved her life on that brutal and sad day. They had so much to talk about. Margarita called the kitchen via the intercom and asked to have her daughter, Este, and her boyfriend, Herny, come to the office for a minute. Both Antonio and Margarita had told their children of their childhood love they had and had never forgotten and how they had promised their love to each other.

Herny and Este came into the room and were surprised to see Antonio and Margelina holding hands. Este noticed the pendent right away, and she said: "Mom, what beautiful pendent; I had never seen it before."

"I did not have it before," she said.

Margarita said: "Remember when I told you about my childhood love and how it impacted my life? This is Antonio, my childhood love. We have been in love with each other since we were six years old. We had lost touch with each other, and now we found each other. He is Herny's father."

"I am so happy to meet you," said Este, in her own loving way, then she gave him a big hug and a kiss on the cheek.

"That is so incredible," said Herny.

"I know we have a lot to catch up on," said Margarita, "but I am the host of the party, and we must go out for a minute."

At the party room, Herny asked for a quiet moment. The room was silenced. He was holding Este's hand, and he said: "I want to take this opportunity to introduce to you my father, Antonio. He lives in Berkley, and I don't think any of you have had an opportunity to meet him." Then he said, "Dad, come on up." Antonio stood next to his son. Herny grabbed Antonio by the hand, raised it up, and said: "He has been my inspiration since I was born. Everything I am is thanks to him. He brought with him his childhood love." Then he said, "Margelina, come on up." She came up and held Antonio's hand.

Margelina told her daughter to go ahead with the party and have a blast.

She was going with Antonio where they could be alone and could talk.

She asked for her limousine to be brought around, and Margarita and Antonio went to his hotel. They started kissing in the car. This woke up the passion they had always had for each other. They got to the hotel, and for the first time, they made passionate love.

Later, Margarita was lying on Antonio's shoulder. She started to cry and said: "You are probably wondering who Este's father is." She went on to say, "You remember the humiliating and violent experience I had when Raul took away all my dignity, my virginity that I had reserved for you, how he raped me in such a violent way? He left me pregnant. No one has ever touched me since. I have been saving it all for you. I had this feeling I would find you. I had hoped that someday we would find each other, and now it is all worthwhile. Though I was so hurt, I thought the pain in my heart would never go away, until I had Este, who has accompanied me ever since. I thought the only children I would ever have would be with you, but Este has been a blessing to me."

⸺⸻⟫⟪⸻⸺

Antonio told her how he challenged Raul to a duel and had put a bullet right through his head. "He hurt me to the core. He hurt the one person I loved most, my Margarita." They both held each other and cried together. Margarita remembered how her family had treated her so bad, but then she had an opportunity to come to America. She said, "I thought it was best to let you live with Britana and have a home without my interference."

Antonio said: "Remember when I was a boy, I always told you that when I grew up I was going to marry you? It took me a long time to grow up. So now, Margarita, you hold my heart in your hands. You have always been the one that had my heart. I want to ask you, will you marry me?"

"Antonio," she said, "we have always loved each other, and long ago we pledged our love for each other. That has never changed for me. Though we have gone through a lot, that bond that we made as children will never break. It cemented us for life. When you kissed me that one time, you sealed my heart, and it has never permitted anyone else to enter. And now, we have these two beautiful kids that we love so much, and they will always be part of our family.

I got to go," said Margarita. "I can't let Este think that I stayed out all night with you. She is a very special girl. She told me that she wants to be a virgin when she marries Herny, and after that, she said, 'He will not only have my heart and my love, but he will also have my body, and he will go where no one else has ever been before,' she said. I am very proud of her. I have been a single mother all these years, but she did okay."

Antonio replied, "I am sure it has to do with the great example you have been as a mother."

Margarita tells Antonio: "I'll see you at the house tomorrow at eleven o'clock. I'll send the car to pick you up. I will ask the kids to be there for a private time together. We have a lot to explain."

Antonio said: "I think they need to know our history, but there are some things that maybe we shouldn't tell them, at least not until our relationship with them has been better established."

Then, Margarita's tears fell again, and she said: "Este already knows. She wanted to know who her father was, and I had to tell her the truth. She cried every day for a long time, but she got over it. I am sure she has told Herny. She tells him everything. They have been involved with an evangelical church that has really helped them both to be better. Anyway, I got to go, I'll see you at the house at eleven."

Antonio was looking through his clothes to see what he was going to wear. He looked into his small jewelry box where he kept his cufflinks. He found the precious stone that Margarita had given him so long ago. He placed it on top of the counter to take with him when he visits Margarita.

The next day at Margarita's house, the big TVs were showing college football games. Margarita had prepared a great brunch, and after they ate, they went into the family room. Antonio said: "There are so many thigs that we need to share with you."

Margarita said: "We grew up together. Antonio is from a royal family in Spain. My family worked for them."

Antonio then said: "I fell in love with Margarita when she was six years old. Though my mother did not approve, I loved to play with the neighborhood kids. That was when I saw Margarita singing and dancing on the porch in front of her house. She was so beautiful, so graceful, so full of life and energy, I couldn't help it; I fell in love with her there and then on the spot. I remember, when I was nine years old, I told her I was going to marry her when we grew up. We were best friends, and we loved being with each other. As we grew older, our relationship improved. Unfortunately, not because we wanted to but destiny took us our separate ways. I married your dear mom. It was sad that you had to see the terrible accident that took her life. Life goes on. It has been a real miracle that we were able to find each other again." He said to Este, "I have asked your mom to marry me, and she has accepted."

"I am so glad," said Margarita, "that though we have gone through troublesome times, here we have an opportunity to have a family together, and I think the best is yet to come. And now, we can even have some grandchildren to spoil."

The two kids went into the backyard, and Antonio reached into his pocket and said, "I got to show you something that is precious to me." He took out the beautiful crystalline stone that Margarita had given him. He said: "Do you remember this?"

"Oh Antonio, you kept this all these years."

"Of course," he said. "This is very precious to me."

The next day, Antonio told Margarita that there was someone he wanted her to meet. He told her about his brave friend Jim who had given his life for his country during the rescue effort in the Philippines.

"Jim had been my very best friend since I came into the military. We knew each other well. I just can't get over losing him. Just before he died, while we were in Vietnam, we had a few hours to rest, and he told me about the great love he had for Peggy.

"He asked me why I had not married after all these years of being alone. He then began telling me about the great romance that still burned between him and Peggy, after all these years of being married.

"He gave me a course in romance. He told me that the first time he saw Peggy, they were both in college attending a dance. 'We were both with a different date and in a different group,' he said. 'Our eyes met, just for a second, and I felt the connection, and I knew she did too.

I watched her all night. I saw her laugh and dance and smile and walk with such grace. I was fascinated with her smile, her poise, and her every movement. Our eyes would cross from time to time, and the spark would be there again and again.' They talked without saying a word. 'Every movement she made opened the door to my heart, but I had to get to know her before I surrendered all of my heart to her. She seemed very beautiful but simple and kind and friendly, and all eyes were on her. Her laughter and her smile filled the room.'

"'Time passed,' he said, 'and I knew I had to find out if she really was the girl of my dreams. From time to time, I would see her on campus with her boyfriend, and every time I saw her, I liked her more, and it was obvious that she was not happy with her boyfriend. Though he was the captain of the football team, I could tell there was something missing. He was very loud and conceded and wanted all the attention all of the time. He was just the opposite to her.

"'One day, I caught up with her, as she was walking to her car. I knew she liked me. I had felt that spark each time our eyes met, and I knew she felt it too. When I caught up with her, I could tell there was something wrong; she was sad. I said hello; I introduced myself. She told me she was Peggy. I knew she was always smiling, but this time she appeared sad. I said, "Where is your beautiful smile?'

"'She said: 'I don't know why I am sad; he certainly is not worth it.' "'What do you mean?' I asked

"'I just broke up with my boyfriend; he has been cheating on me all this time. He does not want a nice decent girl like me, and I am certainly not going to give him what he wants. There are lots of girls that are willing to give him what he wants, but I am not one of them.'

"'I said to her: It's Friday night; I want to see your smile again.' I said, 'There is a concert in town. Santana will be playing his guitar. I have two tickets; why don't you join me?'

"'I would love to go,' she said, I love his music.

"'My parents were going to the concert and had bought tickets for the concert. I had to convince them to let me have them. It was easy when I told them I thought I had found the girl of my dreams. As you know, I came from a religious and a very conservative home.

"'That afternoon, I went all over town trying to find the most beautiful red roses to bring to Peggy. She had recovered her beautiful smile.

"'Every step we took getting to know each other made us both realize we were made for each other. A year later, we graduated from college, and we got married. She was a virgin when we got married, and to be honest with you, I was too. Little by little, we discovered each other, and like every other aspect of our relationship, our sexual experience has always been perfect, like she was made just for me. Over the years, as you know, our love has continued to grow, and now we have this beautiful family that we love and share. I have never been with another woman.

"'So tell me, you are tall and handsome and a great guy,' said Jim, 'tell me why you haven't found a loving woman?'

"'Well,' I said, 'I did, but it's a long story.'

"'Tell me,' he said, 'I want to hear all about it. I want to know why you have never told me about her.'

"'It's a sad story,' I told him, 'and when I think about it, it makes me want to cry.'

"'You can tell me,' he said. 'Was it Herny's mother?' he asked.

"'I had a good relationship with her,' I told him, 'but she was not the one that captured my heart.'

"'We are always talking about so many experiences in our lives, but this is the first time that we really talk about such very personal aspects of our lives,' said Jim.

"I said to him, 'Jim, you know I am the quiet type, and of course, it is difficult for me to talk about my past and my personal life, and it is not because I don't want to share this with you, but you are right; after all these years I want you to know all about my life.'"

"'You know I was born in Spain, but what you don't know is that I was born to a royal family. My world was very different; though I had so much, there was so much of the world we were not permitted to experience.

"'I, too, have a very romantic story to tell, but it did not have a happy ending like yours.

I was brought up in a castle, and when I was six or seven years old, I went out to play, and I saw the six-year-old daughter of one of the workers. She was singing and dancing in front of her house. She was so graceful, so beautiful, so full of life and energy, I gave her my heart there and then. Her name was Margarita. We made a loving friendship that got stronger over the years. As you did with Peggy, I loved her beautiful smile, her gentleness, her kindness towards others, and as the years went by, we promised each other our eternal love.

"'What I did not know was that, when I was just a little boy, my parents had made an arrangement for me to marry my first cousin Britana, Henry's mother. It broke Margarita's heart, and mine too.'

"'Wow, what a story,' said Jim.

"'While working for my family, and shortly after my marriage to Britana, one of my royal friends violently raped Margarita. It broke my heart. After that, and without my knowledge, her family was dismissed from their job. I have not seen her since. I did, however, challenge my friend who raped her to a duel, and I was lucky enough to put a bullet through his head.'

"'Now I understand why you are such a good shot,' said Jim. No doubt you are the best in our unit. I guess I understand better now that you told me the story of why you have remained single all these years.'"

Antonio said to Margarita, "Little did we know that one day later Jim would be dead, and now I am glad we shared this moment together. I am so sad you will never meet him."

Antonio took Margarita to meet Peggy and her family. Peggy knew right away who Margelina was. She had seen some of her movies. Margelina said: "I am so sad to hear what happened to Jim. I know he took a bullet to save my life. I am very grateful. Antonio told me that he will be receiving the Medal of Honor. I know that will not bring him back. There is nothing I can say that will take the pain you have in your heart, but as Antonio said, we will always be a part of your family."

"Life is so sad," said Antonio. "Remember Nelly?" he asked Margarita. "You mean Castro's girlfriend? I remember they loved each other," said Margarita.

"Yes, that's her. I accidently ran into her in Granada years ago. She was raped by Raul also. She told me her whole story; it made me cry. You know the man that was beheaded in front of you? That was Nelly's son. Raul was his father."

"That is incredible," said Margarita.

Antonio said: "I did not know what had happened before we got to the compound that terrible night, but after the military debriefing and interrogating apparently all that were there, they sent me a report of just what happened that sad night."

"I was interrogated, too," said Margarita. "I was desperate to tell them my terrible ordeal of what happened that whole trip, especially that night."

Antonio said: "I didn't know it was Nelly's son that had been beheaded until I got this letter sent by Cardinal Romero from the Catholic Church in the Philippines. Here. I'll read it to you:

"Honorable and Distinguished Cornel Antonio Del Rey:

"I first want to salute you and your men, who put their lives on the line to save and protect and give hope to others. Others whose hope turned into terror and despair.

"The trauma they went through that night will impact them all their lives. I know this will be an unforgettable night of horror for you and your men as well.

"I have asked the Lord to bless all of your courageous men who try to undue the unjust and bring justice. It is sad for us that we had to resolve this violence with violence. I know the Lord will judge us with mercy and look into our hearts in the quest for justice and honor and freedom and peace.

"I am so sad that one of your men, Lieutenant Coronel James White, had to give his life. I visited with his widow, Peggy, and the children. Their sadness I could not console, and my heart and prayers will always be with them.

"We also lost a hero and a great man of God that night, Padre David. He was a courageous and a great man of God. He gave his life to save others. He was savagely and brutally murdered. Crushing the spirits of all present, bringing horror and terror and hopelessness.

"When I opened the file of Padre David, I found a sad and incredible story that I want to share with you.

"His mother was raped when she was just fourteen years old. She was thrown out of her house because she was pregnant. She apparently tried to find a life with some relatives. No one could help her, and she became a single mother, working at night as a prostitute to survive. The boy, David, grew up in the gutter, without structure or a role model and with very bad influences that molded his young mind into drugs and a life of crime, mostly petty theft and traffic of drugs.

"While living on the street under a bridge, he overdosed on narcotics and severely injured his brain.

"Our Padre Francisco made it his project to pray every day for David. He documented the story that is now in his file. When he discovered that Father David had died in such barbaric way, he sent us the story of David.

When David overdosed and was in a coma, Padre Francisco made David his project. No one ever came to see David. He apparently was an orphan, until, one day, his mother appeared.

"She told Padre Francisco the whole story. Miraculously, David woke up. He was taken in by the Catholic Church. He became a priest and was sent to the Philippines as a missionary where he started a mission with a church, a school, an orphanage, and a place to help the poor, the unfortunate, and those in despair. He was loved by all who knew him. The world has lost a great man of God. We will miss him dearly.

"I wanted to reach out to you and let you know that we are in deep sorrow and pray for you and your men every day. I hope that, with the grace of God, your wounded hearts will heal, and though you will never forget and you will always feel the pain, you will realize that life will go on.

"May you receive the spirit and grace and the blessings of God, and may you find peace. You and your men forever will be in our hearts, and in our prayers.

"Respectfully yours, Cardinal Romero.

"I met up with Nelly in Granada years ago. She introduced me to her son David. He was twelve years old. He was into drugs and had dishonorable, bad friends. I tried to take him home with me, but he would not come. It was so sad."

"That is really something," said Margarita. "That means that this priest, David, is Este's brother. Wow, how terrible. I don't know how I am going to handle this with Este. I don't want to open old wounds that brought her world down to her knees years ago. Still, she might find comfort in the thought that her brother, after making life-threatening mistakes, after a terrible childhood, found his path and became an honorable and decent man that made the ultimate sacrifice to save us and others."

"All this time, I have been so involved with my profession, trying to forget my pain of having to lose you, and there you were, right under my nose all this time," said Antonio.

"When I talked to Nelly, it made me wonder how you had survived after the sad and violent rape. I often cried wondering where you were. I tried to find you. I found your family, and they told me you had left. I could hear the hatred in your father's voice. It broke my heart, but now here we are, and I have decided to dedicate the rest of my life to work with you and your project and see how we can improve it. I want to spend the rest of my life with Herny and Este, and, of course, you and our future grandchildren. I have never forgotten you and thought about you every day," said Antonio. "I always wondered what happened to you, and now, for the first time, I really have the home that I dreamt about since we were children."